witch
season

WINTER

JEFF MARIOTTE

Simon Pulse
New York London Toronto Sydney

For Maryelizabeth, once again.

▨SIMON PULSE
An imprint of Simon & Schuster
Children's Publishing Division
1230 Avenue of the Americas, New York, NY 10020

Copyright © 2005 by Jeff Mariotte
All rights reserved, including the right of
reproduction in whole or in part in any form.

SIMON PULSE and colophon
are registered trademarks of Simon & Schuster, Inc.

Designed by Ann Zeak
The text of this book was set in Bembo.

Manufactured in the United States of America
First Simon Pulse edition January 2005
10 9 8 7 6 5 4 3 2 1

Library of Congress Control Number 2004108046

ISBN 0-689-86725-5

More to it than met the eye

Who says she gets to make the rules? Scott wondered.

He stayed out of Kerry's view but kept an eye on her. It was only a few minutes until Season showed up and Kerry chased her outside.

He hadn't been able to get close enough to hear, but he could see just fine. They feigned a perfectly friendly conversation, but from Kerry's body language and some of her movements, he knew there was more to it than met the eye. Then Season led Kerry away—straight toward the parking lot. . . .

Season led Kerry to a black Jeep 4X4. Scott ran to the RAV4, jumped in, and cranked the engine. By the time Season was leaving the parking lot, he was three cars behind. He opened his cell phone and dialed.

"Hello?" she answered a moment later. "Scott?"

"Brandy, listen, I know you don't want me calling you, but this is important. Season Howe just kidnapped Kerry."

As the seasons change, so does Kerry. . . .
Check out the other installments
in the Witch Season series:

Summer

Fall

Winter

And coming soon from Simon Pulse:

Spring

Huge thanks to those people who helped make this one happen, including Michelle, Bethany, and Amanda; Howard and Mara; Tara, Cindy, and the usual crew of friends and colleagues who keep me sane: Chris, Jack, Scott, et al.

I was ready to run.

Not that I brought much with me to Mother Blessing's that I need to take away, but there are a few things—my old red-checked tennies, a couple of sweatshirts and some jeans I've grown attached to, my stash of cash, this laptop, BoBo the clown doll, and some of Daniel's journals—that I don't want to leave behind.

By now I know my way through the swamp, so I'm not that concerned about provisions for the trip—no need to weigh myself down with energy bars or anything. But when I leave here this time, I'm never coming back. I don't want to forget anything that I might want later.

And, truth? I don't want to leave anything that Mother Blessing might be able to use to track me down.

But by the time I threw the few things I want to take into a duffel bag, Mother Blessing came out of her room and started wheeling around the house, slamming doors and cursing and shouting out— certainly for my benefit—things like "I can't believe what a liar that Season Howe is!"

I was hoping to get out of the house before she

emerged from seclusion, so I'd be gone well before she knew I was missing. Because, let's face it, Thanksgiving hadn't exactly turned out like I'd planned. The groceries I had bought were still in my van—the turkey no doubt well thawed by now—at Edgar Brandvold's place, but Edgar had been murdered. I thought by Season Howe, since she seems to make a habit of killing people I know, including Daniel Blessing, Mother Blessing's son and the man I loved. But now everything I thought I knew about Mother Blessing and Season has been turned upside down, with the new information that Season is apparently Mother's mother. And, according to Season, there are other things Mother Blessing hasn't told me as well, which feed into certain questions I have run up against. Such as, which one was really the mega-destructo queen who trashed Slocumb, Virginia, three hundred years ago?

Confusion reigns. All I know for sure is that nothing is for sure. Maybe Mother Blessing killed Edgar to make me think Season had done it. Maybe Mother Blessing destroyed Slocumb and then sent her sons—Abraham and Daniel, both now deceased at Season's hands—after Season, to hide her own guilt.

Almost certainly Mother Blessing has been less

than honest with me. And also almost certainly, she knows that since our confrontation with Season I am suspicious of her. The combination, it seems to me, is a dangerous one, which is why I really want to get gone.

But now she's banging around the house, and if I leave my room she'll see me. I'm trying to wait her out, hoping she'll give up and go to bed, and then I can scram.

The Great Dismal Swamp at night isn't exactly my favorite place. Dark, full of bugs and gators and snakes and the occasional bear. But right now, it beats the heck out of staying in this house an instant longer than I absolutely have to.

More later.

K.

1

Mother Blessing's door slammed again.

She'd been doing this for an hour—coming out of her room, rolling around the halls, the rubber wheels of her scooter squeaking on hardwood floors, then going back in. Slamming doors like an eight-year-old throwing a tantrum.

Except most eight-year-olds weren't potentially lethal.

Is she in for the night this time? Kerry wondered. *Or just for a couple of minutes?*

The answer could, literally, be that proverbial matter of life and death.

Gotta get out of here gotta get out of here gotta get out . . .

The door opened. Wheels squeaked. Barely

breathing, Kerry closed her laptop and listened. Mother Blessing had stopped shouting so much, but she was muttering something under her breath that Kerry couldn't make out. Panic gripped Kerry for a moment—the scooter was coming all the way down the hall to the guest room, the room in which Kerry had spent much of the autumn, learning magic at Mother Blessing's side. Given what had transpired earlier—Season Howe informing Kerry, in front of Mother Blessing, that most of what she had been told about the mutual history of the two witches was wrong—Kerry couldn't help feeling that Mother Blessing would not be in a jovial mood when next they met.

Kerry had power. She knew that now. She had learned well, and magic seemed to come naturally to her.

But she was nowhere near Mother Blessing's level. If the old witch decided that it would be advantageous now to just take Kerry out, there would be little Kerry could do to dissuade her.

She held her breath for several seconds, but then the scooter's wheels squeaked again as Mother Blessing turned away from her door.

Kerry heard the door to Mother Blessing's room open, and then slam shut again.

Is she working up her courage? Kerry thought. *Why? What kind of threat could I be to her?*

Sounds from Mother Blessing's room filtered down the hallway to her. They could have been the sounds of Mother Blessing preparing for bed—it was past ten now, her typical bedtime—but rain still hammered the roof, and it was hard to be sure.

Kerry waited another half hour. The minutes dragged by like days, weeks. Finally the noises from Mother Blessing's room died out.

Kerry was convinced that if she stayed, tomorrow would bring a confrontation with the old witch that she would probably not survive. She had successfully dodged it for tonight, probably because Mother Blessing herself was so weakened from the afternoon's magical battle with Season that she hadn't wanted to force the issue.

By morning Mother Blessing would have regained her strength. She would want to discuss the things Season had said—a discussion that would lead inexorably to Kerry's concerns that she had been lied to since arriving at the cabin in the swamp earlier in the fall. If Kerry lived long enough, she would most likely accuse Mother Blessing of having lied to her own sons as well—of sending them off to kill a witch they didn't even know was their grandmother.

If Kerry was to get another day older, she had to leave tonight.

She had been ready for hours now, but she waited still longer. She wanted Mother Blessing to be deeply asleep. The old house's floors could creak when she walked across them, and the last thing she wanted was for Mother Blessing to wake up and find her on her way out. That would precipitate the very confrontation Kerry was trying to avoid.

Every minute was torture, every tick of the guest room wall clock agonizing. She almost took out her laptop to write some more in her journal, but then stopped herself. She wanted to be alert, aware, in case Mother Blessing woke up. Losing herself in her diaries was a distraction she couldn't afford. She couldn't even pace, for fear that her steps would wake the witch whose house she shared.

Midnight passed. *The witching hour,* she

thought. Except for Mother Blessing, who, witch or no, almost always slept right through it.

But then, I guess I'm a witch too, now. Not as skilled and practiced as Mother Blessing or Season Howe. But if being a witch is defined by doing witchcraft, then I am one. So I can observe the witching hour all by my lonesome.

She waited, and let Mother Blessing sleep.

When the clock ticked over to twelve-thirty, Kerry decided she had waited long enough. Her bag was already packed. She tied her long black hair back with a leather thong, pulled a coat from the closet, wrapped it around herself against the cold and rain she knew were waiting outside in the dark, and opened her door. Her room was at the end of a hallway, and she had to go past Mother Blessing's room to get out of the house. She stepped as lightly as she could manage, holding the duffel away from her body so it didn't rub against her jeans. In her other hand she carried boots, which she would only pull on when she was at the door.

She had almost made it when Mother Blessing's bedroom door opened, spilling light, and her scooter nosed out into the hall.

Kerry's heart leapt into her throat as she spun around to see Mother Blessing glaring at her over her oxygen mask. The woman's breathing was labored, her voice muffled when she spoke.

"Where are y'all goin'?"

This was precisely what Kerry had hoped to avoid. She hadn't wanted a confrontation or a scene. She simply wanted to vanish, as she had from Northwestern University when she had decided that she wanted to come here, to the swamp, to have Mother Blessing teach her magic so she could take revenge on Season Howe.

That worked out great, huh? she thought.

Now, facing Mother Blessing's glare, Kerry delivered the line she'd been practicing. "I'm . . . uh . . . going after Season," she said. "She can't be too far away yet."

Mother Blessing just stared, her breathing Darth Vaderesque through the mask.

"You've taught me a lot," Kerry went on. Her mind screamed at her to *shut up, already!*, but her mouth didn't comply. "I think it's time to move on, though. Got to stay on Season's trail until I can kill her."

Mother Blessing stared. Finally she spoke again. "I don't think that's a good idea."

"Yeah, well, I kind of do," Kerry returned, defiance starting to rise in her. "So, thanks a lot and all, but I've got to get going."

"No."

Obviously conversation wasn't a good idea. Kerry dropped the duffel, tugged on her boots, picked it up again. Another glance at Mother Blessing, who was rolling in her direction now, her mouth scowling behind the oxygen mask, and Kerry stepped out the door.

"No!" she heard Mother Blessing cry behind her.

Kerry slammed the door and ran through driving rain to the shallow-bottomed skiff Mother Blessing kept for traveling out of the swamp. She hurled the duffel in, pushed it off the bank, climbed in, and shoved the oars into the oarlocks. As she started to row, she glanced back toward the house—which always looked like a tumbledown old trapper's cabin from the outside—and saw Mother Blessing silhouetted in the doorway, her arms raised in the air.

That, she thought, terrified, *is not good.*

But with strength that came from working

hard around the swamp for weeks, she dipped the oars into the murky water and pulled.

It was impossible to tell where the water ended and the trees began, and just as hard to know where the tops of the trees merged with the sky. Moonlight filtered through only in rare spots. Trees were a wall of black against black. The toads, crickets, night birds, the rare and piercing howl of a bobcat, were all but drowned out by the pounding rain and the occasional crack of thunder, adding to Kerry's confusion and disorientation.

At this moment, however, she was more concerned with steering the shallow boat between the trees and not grounding it than with direction. She needed to find her way through the honeycomb of canals and creeks to someplace where she could catch a ride far away from here, but it wouldn't do her any good to get away from Mother Blessing if she killed herself trying. Since she wasn't sure who had killed Edgar Brandvold, or why—and since she had told Mother Blessing that she'd left the minivan at his place when she arrived and found Edgar murdered—she didn't want to risk going back there. Mother Blessing had not been happy about her leaving, and if she were going to try to stop Kerry—or to send her simulacra to do that—the van would be the obvious place to start.

A flash of lightning momentarily illuminated a barricade of tree trunks right before her. Kerry put her oars to water and pulled backward, trying to brake herself, to lessen the impact of imminent collision. At what she figured was the last moment, she raised an oar and thrust it out before her to stave off the bank. She felt the oar hit the bank, felt the boat stop in the water just before it rammed.

But when she tried to lower the oar to the water again, something held it fast. She yanked at it, but to no avail. Whatever had her oar wasn't letting go—and, she realized, it was drawing her in toward the bank.

Simulacra? Kerry wondered. If she'd just snagged it on something, she would be able to free it, she was certain. She had a flashlight with her but hadn't bothered to use it, since it would have meant taking a hand off the oars. Now, though, she released the stuck oar and grabbed for the flashlight, at the top of her duffel bag. She drew it out and flicked it on.

Something had her oar, all right, but it wasn't one of Mother Blessing's manufactured men. It was a baldcypress root sticking out from the bank. It had wound itself three times around the end of the oar and was waving it like a magician with a wand.

Kerry knew the root could not have grabbed the oar like that without help. Mother Blessing was trying to stop her—and using the swamp to do it!

While she watched, another root snaked toward her. She ducked away from its grasp. It came again, and she bashed it with the flashlight.

That wouldn't hold it for long. She clicked off the light and jammed it back into the duffel, zipping the bag closed to keep out the rain. With her remaining oar—no way would she be able to fight the tree for the other one, not while it had dozens of roots that might attack her—she pulled hard against the water, alternating sides of the skiff to keep on an even course.

She was only a few yards away from where she'd lost her oar when she felt something damp brush her face. *A spider web,* she thought, *or some low-hanging Spanish moss.* Either was possible here. She swiped at it with one hand—and it snaked around her wrist, pulling tighter as she tried to tug away.

Kerry screamed and yanked her arm. Whatever it was—she thought she felt leaves on it, like a vine of some kind—wouldn't let go. She swung at it with the oar but couldn't break its grip. It started to lift her up out of the boat.

Panic threatened to overtake her as she struggled against the vine. Another one wrapped around her waist and tightened there, like a belt cinching up. Her free right hand dropped to her own belt, but the knife she wore sometimes in the swamp wasn't there, and she remembered tossing it into the duffel when she'd packed.

When the next vine looped around her throat, she thought it was all over. It closed tightly on her, cutting off her airway. By now she was mostly out of the skiff, could feel with her feet that it was drifting away from her.

Which was when she remembered that she was a witch too.

A kind of calm settled over Kerry's racing mind. Mother Blessing was turning the swamp against her through magic. But she wasn't the only magic-user around. She had taught Kerry quite a few tricks—but more important, she had taught her philosophies and systems. She may not have known a specific spell to free herself from living vines, but that didn't mean she was defenseless.

With her throat closed off and one hand out of commission, speaking the old tongue and making the correct gestures was tricky. But she managed to croak out the word *"Kalaksit!"* and curl the fingers of her free hand toward her palm while splaying the thumb out. White flame crackled at her fingertips. She felt herself relaxing even more, letting the now-familiar sensation wash over her—the thrill of power, the rush of magic. Raindrops sizzled against her fire. Aiming by the light the flickering flames provided, she pointed at the vine that encircled her throat and willed the fire into a narrow, straight blast. It cut the vine as keenly as a laser.

Next came the one around her waist, and then her arm. Kerry dropped back down to the skiff, but unbalanced, she went over backward, landing faceup in the shallow water. She allowed herself a bitter smile. It hardly mattered; she was already drenched from the rain. The flames at her fingertips died in the creek, but that was okay. She could always make more.

She climbed back into the skiff, found the remaining oar, and started to row.

Okay, then, she thought as she churned the water, driving the boat quickly up the creek. *Mother Blessing is definitely opposed to me leaving. Don't know yet if she's homicidal about it, but she's obviously serious.*

Kerry rowed and rowed. Her arms started to ache, her shoulders and back protesting from the effort. The rain gave up, and by the time light started to show itself, patches of silver and pink visible through the leafy ceiling to the east, she knew something was wrong. She had been making for the old Slocumb site—the blasted, cursed township Season and Mother Blessing had once shared—and she should have reached it within a few hours. Navigation had been difficult in the dark, but even so. . . .

More light filtered in through the trees and Kerry saw a bank that she recognized, with roots reaching through the bluff of clay and diving into the water, a big, pale mushroom sticking out of one like a dinner plate wedged halfway in. She had seen that bank at least an hour or two before, on one of the occasions when she'd taken out her flashlight to gauge her path. She was positive she hadn't been rowing in circles—the swamp wasn't so well organized that one could even do that intentionally. Which could only mean that the swamp itself was shifting, changing itself around in an effort to keep her here.

What if it isn't Mother Blessing? Kerry wondered as the icy hands of fear gripped her again. *What if it's Season—or the swamp itself? What if it doesn't want me to leave? Will I ever get out then?*

But Kerry Profitt was the Bulldog, she reminded herself. It didn't matter who—or what—was trying to keep her here. The only thing that mattered was that she was determined to get out, and so she would. She drifted past the familiar bank. Now that the sun had come up, she knew which direction east was. Slocumb was to the east, and a highway ran alongside the Great Dismal in that direction. She would find an exit, at one spot or another.

Kerry had traveled maybe another half mile when the water started moving faster under her boat. It took her in the direction she wanted to go, so she let the current carry her, using the oar only to keep herself away from the banks. A family of feral pigs watched her race by from a bluff; crows and three snowy egrets took flight at her rapid approach.

Then the creek widened, and ahead she could see where it joined with a broader canal. By now she was completely lost—she was nowhere she had ever been before, or, more likely, the swamp had never been configured in just this way before. She put the oar to water to help ease herself into the canal, but when her smaller tributary hit the larger one, the water there rushed faster than she had ever seen water move here. It was like a river's rapids, not like the near-stagnant swamp water she was used to. Her heart raced as she tried to steady the shallow skiff, but the little boat was no match for the sudden flow.

Water roared in her ears and splashed ahead of the skiff, and Kerry found herself spinning around and around, the oar useless to stop her. Then the tiny craft was hurled against a jagged bank, where it splintered. Kerry snatched up her duffel bag as the water rushed in, and hurled it up onto the bank. The water in the swamp was rarely deep, but things lived in it that she didn't want to encounter if she could help it—water moccasins and alligators foremost among them. Grabbing exposed roots, she pulled herself onto dry land, where she sat down hard and watched the boards that had once been the skiff separate and float away.

The waterways were the highways of the swamp, Kerry knew. There were trails on land, but they were mostly animal paths, unsuited for anything as big and ungainly as a human being. Kerry was slender enough for most trails, but when they wound underneath spreading ferns and fallen trunks, they could be impassable even for her.

Still, it didn't look like she had much choice now. She headed vaguely east until she found a faint track and then followed it.

And still Mother Blessing wasn't done with her, she discovered. After maybe a mile or so, Kerry discovered that she was being followed.

She heard the chuffing sound of a big cat first and froze in place. Slowly, carefully, she turned and looked back down her trail, and after a few minutes a bobcat showed itself, its strange golden eyes fixed on her. But the bobcat wasn't alone— a black bear parted the brush and stood beside the feline. Kerry knew that would never happen in nature—only Mother Blessing's intercession could have made those two creatures into allies.

Knowing that didn't make Kerry feel any better about it. Either one, bear or bobcat, could do a lot of damage if it attacked her. Both acting together, impossible as it was to imagine, could easily tear her to shreds.

She could defend herself, of course. But the idea of hurting either of those animals, forced against their own natures to cooperate in her destruction, was repellent to Kerry.

Fighting the tremor in her knees, the urge to run, she turned away slowly, showing them her back. She then continued down the trail she had found, heading into the morning sun, moving at a steady clip—not running, but not slow.

Behind her, she heard the animals keeping pace.

To panic, to run, would certainly bring them both charging down on her. This way they remained at bay, tracking without charging, while she tried to think of a way to reverse the spell that had enchanted them.

No such reversal came to mind. Kerry was exhausted. She hadn't slept since yesterday morning, Thanksgiving, which seemed a lifetime ago, and then the battle with Season, the effort of rowing all night—it was no wonder answers weren't coming to her as quickly as they might have.

Finally an idea occurred to her. The animals had been set on her trail by Mother Blessing, no doubt with malicious intent. They hadn't attacked her yet, but Kerry was convinced that they would when their instincts told them she was a threat or when she tried to run. She didn't know how she could alter the programming, but she was pretty sure she could change their target. She stopped, then spun around, facing them again. Speaking a couple of the magic words she had learned, gesturing with both hands, she pointed toward a nearby puddle and raised the water from it. With the water that now hovered in the air between herself and the animals, she sculpted the image of Mother Blessing—all three hundred pounds or more of her, complete with scooter, oxygen tanks, and beehive hairdo. She tried to look into the eyes of each animal, and she drove into their minds the concept that this person was their enemy, their mutual target. Finally she hurled the water sculpture at them. Bear and cat both flinched away, but it splashed against them, harmless but soaking.

When it was over, both creatures regarded Kerry almost casually, and then looked this way and that, up and down the path. They were no longer fixed on her, she believed. She waved her arms at them, and they backed away, turning and going back the way they had come.

Kerry didn't know how long Mother Blessing's spell would last—or how long her own would, for that matter. But if it held, and if these two unlikely companions found their way to Mother Blessing's cabin, the old witch was in for an unpleasant surprise.

The path twisted and turned, widening here, narrowing to almost nothingness there. Always it led east, which was where Kerry had decided salvation lay anyway. So she stayed with it as best she could.

In another hour or so, she could hear the rush of cars on the highway. She struggled to place her weary feet. The duffel was so heavy she was regretting having brought it. The world no longer seemed to conspire against her—when vines snatched at her ankles or thorns tore at her sleeves, they were simply doing what vines and thorns naturally did. But she was almost ready to admit defeat anyway, not sure how long she could continue the hike. The sound of cars perked her up a little. But they were still at some distance, with plenty of thick swamp between her and them.

She drove herself on. When her mind started to wander, when she began to lose her focus, to fall asleep on her feet, she reminded herself of Mace Winston, whom Season had killed back in San Diego during the summer. That summer had changed everything for her—had taken a life that was moving in one direction, as surely as the creek that had carried her skiff, and spun it around just like the canal had done the little boat. Summer had introduced her to Daniel Blessing, three hundred years old and, as it turned out, the love of her life. She allowed the memory of his smile, kind and genuine, to fill her for a moment. It brought her a few seconds of peace, reminded her why she was doing all this. He was the handsomest man she'd ever seen—centuries old, sure, but witchcraft, she had learned, was the original Botox and didn't even involve needles or deadly germs.

But the summer had also brought Season Howe into her life, and Season had killed Mace, and later Daniel. Then, during the fall, when Kerry was in the swamp learning from Daniel's mother, Season had apparently tracked down Rebecca in Santa Cruz, and Josh in Las Vegas. Josh hadn't survived the encounter. The only ones remaining from the summer house in La Jolla were herself, Rebecca, Brandy, and Scott.

Finally Season had shown up here, in the Great Dismal. Where it had all started, so many years before. Here she hadn't been able to defeat Mother Blessing and Kerry, but neither had they been able to triumph over her. It almost didn't matter—the things Season had said were enough to make Kerry rethink everything that had happened since August.

She had been motivated by thoughts of revenge against Season ever since Daniel had died.

Now it wasn't so much revenge that spurred her on, although that was still a factor. Now—just since yesterday afternoon—what Kerry discovered she wanted most in the world was the truth. She wanted to know who had destroyed Slocumb. She wanted to understand the relationship between Season and Mother Blessing, wanted to know what Daniel and his brother Abraham had known about it.

That quest, instead of just simple revenge, kept her putting one foot before the other, ducking branches, dodging thorns. She tried to remain alert, worried that Mother Blessing would have turned the swamp against her in ways she hadn't encountered yet. But her eyes grew bleary and her concentration flagged.

Until finally she topped a low rise and saw, at the bottom of a weed-choked slope, the highway she sought. Highway 17 ran north-south here, along the edge of the Great Dismal Swamp. It would take her away—away from Mother Blessing, away from Season Howe.

It was so beautiful, that strip of lined asphalt, that Kerry thought she would cry.

2

Kerry didn't know exactly what she looked like, but she was pretty sure she was a horrific mess. A full night and all morning in the swamp, in the rain, falling out of the boat—all after an epic battle—would do it to anyone, she decided. She hadn't spent time on her appearance since yesterday morning, when she'd cleaned up and brushed her hair and even put on a little makeup because she was going into Deep Creek to do the holiday feast shopping.

If she were driving and spotted herself hitchhiking, she would lock her doors and speed up.

She couldn't do much about her physical appearance—not without a shower and a hair-brush and maybe a new wardrobe. But that didn't mean she had to let passing motorists know what she really looked like. Casting a glamour was one of the first tricks Mother Blessing had taught her. It was basic, and while it didn't necessarily have anything to do with the more common definition of "glamour," there was no reason it couldn't apply. She decided she would look like a clean-cut, friendly student, in the swamp to study its biology or something. She visualized what she wanted people to see, changing as little of herself as possible. The muddy, torn coat became a clean sweatshirt with a UVA logo on it, the shredded jeans were crisp and new, the fouled, mud-caked boots were shiny green duck boots. She imagined her hair as she liked it best, loose and flowing in the breeze, raven-dark and fine. She visualized herself only lightly made up, her natural porcelain complexion undisguised, her green eyes almost luminous. As a finishing touch she imagined a faint scent of lilac, instead of the swamp mud and sweat she really smelled like.

Once that was accomplished, she ventured out to the edge of the roadway and stuck out her thumb when the next batch of vehicles raced up the highway. She wanted to go north, toward Portsmouth and Norfolk, and points beyond. But either of those nearby cities would do for a start.

Six months before, Kerry would have been petrified to even consider hitchhiking anywhere. She still understood that it was not the safest mode of transport, particularly for a young woman. But compared with what she had survived in the past twenty-four hours alone, it was a piece of cake.

The third car that came along stopped for her. A man in his early thirties drove, a pretty woman by his side. In the back was an array of photography equipment—camera bags, tripods, backpacks, and the like. The woman rolled down her window as Kerry jogged up to the car.

"Where are you heading?" she asked.

"Portsmouth, I guess," Kerry told her.

"We're going to Newport News," the woman said, "so that's on the way. If you can find a place to sit with all that junk in the back, you're welcome to ride."

"I don't take up much space," Kerry promised. She climbed into the back. The driver pulled back out into the lane, and the woman started to say something else. But the motion of the car on the highway lulled Kerry, and though she tried to listen, within minutes she had slipped into a deep sleep.

The Friday after Thanksgiving is, retail legend has it, the busiest shopping day of the year. Brandy Pearson saw no reason to doubt the conventional wisdom. Her parents lived in Needham, a Boston suburb, and she had foolishly tried to go to one of the town's independent bookstores to find something to read during the Thanksgiving break that wasn't required for one class or other. She didn't have anything particular in mind—she enjoyed chick-lit, legal thrillers, suspense, and the occasional romance, as well as popular biographies, and she figured she could easily find something in one of those categories that caught her eye.

So she fought the bundled-up throngs, trying to peer past anxious shoppers at the covers and spines of the books on the store's shelves. She browsed new hardcover fiction first, picking up and putting back at least a dozen books. She had experienced a lot in the past several months, since San Diego and the discovery that witches were real—and deadly. She had mourned Mace and Josh and even Daniel, who had drawn them all into it. She had broken up with Scott, who had been, for a time, the guy she thought was forever. Now she found that fiction that took some matters too lightly—the existence of the supernatural, life and death, love and hate—didn't appeal to her anymore. She picked up a book with a knife on the cover—she had heard somewhere that knives on book covers were guaranteed sellers—flipped it open, read the cover flap. Then she put it back where she'd found it.

"Do you taste them too?" a voice asked from behind her. "Or just squeeze them to see if they're ripe?"

Half-expecting to see someone she knew, Brandy turned around. But the young man who had spoken was a stranger—*a handsome stranger,* she corrected herself, but a stranger just the same. He was about her age or a little older, early twenties, maybe. His friendly smile revealed even, white teeth. His hair was short, neatly cropped, his eyes were wide and cheerful. His skin was several shades darker than her own, set off nicely by a cream-colored dress shirt underneath his heavy winter coat. Clean blue jeans and expensive leather shoes made up the rest of the ensemble. Brandy had to approve.

"If you take them home too early they just spoil," she replied. "Vine-ripened is always best, at least for hardcovers. Paperbacks you can keep in a bag for a few days if you need to, and they'll usually turn out just fine."

"I see you know a lot about the care and feeding," the man said. "Maybe you can give me a lesson sometime."

Is he asking me out? Brandy wondered. *We just met, like, seconds ago. We haven't met, really. Well, one way to fix that.*

She extended her hand. "I'm Brandy Pearson," she said with a smile. "World-famous expert on book botany."

"Adam Castle," he said, taking her hand in his. His hand was large and warm, and he shook hers with a firm grip and then released it. "Not world famous at all."

"Give it time," she said. "I'm sure you'll find your niche."

"I'm afraid my specialty is a little more mundane. Urban planning."

A browser reaching for a new Dean Koontz novel jostled Brandy. "Nothing wrong with that," she said, sidestepping so as not to take another elbow to the ribs, and glad she wore a heavy woolen pea coat over her lavender turtleneck and black yoga pants. "Especially if you can urbanly plan a shopping experience where there's some kind of consideration for personal space."

The shopper put the Koontz book down, shot Brandy a glare, and said, "Excuse me," as he moved down to the next shelf unit.

Adam laughed. "Ouch. You don't pull any punches, do you, Brandy?"

"Only when there's a good reason to," Brandy replied. "Which, it seems, is pretty rare."

"Yeah, you're right about that, I think," he said. "And to answer your question, yes, I think I do have some interesting ideas about retail spaces. Of course, this is an example of what I like—smaller independent stores, as opposed to big-box chains. But there are ways to situate them, and to organize the insides, that create a more efficient and user-friendly shopping experience, and . . . you were just saying that, right?

You didn't really want to hear my theories."

"Not that they're not fascinating," Brandy assured him. "Because I'm sure they are, in the right setting. I just don't think this is it."

Adam laughed again. Brandy found herself responding to his laughter—it was honest, with a lack of self-consciousness that she found refreshing. She knew virtually nothing about this man except that he was strangely appealing. She wasn't in the market for a relationship, especially so soon after breaking up with Scott. But there was some kind of instant connection going on here, it seemed. This guy was cute, he made her laugh, and he seemed to have a few brains in his head, all of which were qualities that Brandy appreciated.

She wasn't the kind of person who could just fall into a romance, anyway, even if she had been looking for one. She was too analytical for that. She tried to look at every aspect of a person or situation and make up her mind based on the facts as she found them. The fact that she was even thinking in romantic terms, just minutes after seeing Adam's face for the first time in her life, was unusual for her, and she figured that when she took the time to analyze her own reaction she might find that it was meaningful in that context. Her immediate response to him indicated to her that there might be something there worth responding to.

But on a friendship basis only, she decided. *I am not looking for a new boyfriend already.*

Adam seemed to be thinking along similar lines. He ticked his head toward the bookshop's coffee bar, where a few empty tables stood among people reading through magazines, chatting, or working on laptop computers. "Would you like to get something to drink?" he asked her. "And then we can talk about what the right setting might be."

Brandy had to think about the invitation for almost three whole seconds before she accepted.

The Charles River separated Cambridge, home of Harvard University, from Boston. The river wasn't visible from Scott Banner's family home on Marlborough Street in the Back Bay, but one knew it was nearby just the same—its edges choked with ice at this time of year, hardy runners blowing out clouds of steam as they jogged its footpaths.

The house was ridiculously large, Scott had always thought, five stories of red brick on the outside, its roof turreted and dotted with four chimneys. Snow webbed the trees in front of it. Old New England money had paid for the house, and Scott Banner's father—now known as Judge Banner, though he'd spent most of his professional life as a partner at a downtown law firm—was perfectly happy to take full advantage of the privileges life had cast his way.

Scott knew that his gut response might be written off as typical teen rebellion. But even as he relaxed on a leather couch in the media room, watching old movies on the plasma TV, he couldn't help thinking about the millions of hungry people who could be fed for the cost of this one house. His father was a philanthropist who gave heavily to dozens of worthy causes, but Scott had decided that someday when he inherited all of this, he'd sell the house, live a more reasonable lifestyle, and share with the needy the wealth that had been passed down to him.

For now it was a nice place to relax after the Thanksgiving feast of the day before. The grand dining room had been full, with family friends and relatives spilling off the main table, which seated twenty-four, and using two additional tables that had been set up for the overflow. The meal had been huge—again, bringing Scott a rush of guilt over those who got their only Thanksgiving turkey from a shelter, if they even had that option. After dinner the party had split into different rooms: Scott and his older brother Steve had gone into the game room and taken all comers on at the pool table, while others had gone to the media room for football, or onto the patio in back, heated with standing propane warmers, for cigars and brandy.

Last year, he kept remembering, he and Brandy had been together on Thanksgiving, spending part of the day here and part at her family's home in Needham. The contrast had been marked—her parents were well-off, but they had earned it themselves, and their lifestyle was comfortable but not ostentatious. Her family seemed to like him, and his family definitely enjoyed her company. He must have explained thirty times yesterday why she wasn't with him for the meal.

The truth was, he had a hard time figuring it out for himself.

She accused him of secretly longing for Kerry Profitt. And when he was honest with himself, he couldn't really deny that charge. Kerry was a remarkable young woman—beautiful, brave, and resourceful. Of the group of them who had been thrown together in a house during the summer, she had been through the worst of it. Scott's heart had gone out to her, and that, plus the undeniable physical attraction he felt, created the situation that bugged Brandy so.

His brother Steve came into the room, glancing at the movie playing on the big screen. "Can't go wrong with Indy," he said. "Well, maybe except for that middle one."

"That's why I'm on number three," Scott agreed.

Steve sat in a club chair next to Scott's couch. Like Scott, his eyesight was terrible, but unlike Scott he'd been willing to have lasers beamed into his eyes to correct it. He was a little taller than Scott, sandy-haired and tennis-fit. "You've been pretty down last couple of days, little bro," Steve said. "What's up?"

Scott shrugged. There was so much he couldn't tell Steve—about Season Howe, and the friends who had died. "I guess a little class consciousness," he said. "Feeling bad that we're the haves in a world of have-nots."

"Feel free to join the Peace Corps, dude," Steve suggested. They'd had this discussion before.

"Maybe I will," Scott said. With a grin, he added, "You tell Mom."

Steve was six years older than Scott, and they had been close since childhood. In the last couple of years they'd grown apart, largely because they hardly ever saw each other—Scott was busy with Harvard, while Steve was busy climbing the tenure track at Amherst. Even so, it wasn't hard for one brother to tell when the other was hedging something. "Is it Brandy?" Steve asked. "Must've hurt yesterday when people kept asking where she was."

Scott nodded. "Yeah, that's part of it. A big part, I guess. I just miss her a lot, you know?"

"Understood," Steve said. He was married to a girl he'd known since his senior year of high school, so Scott was pretty sure he had no recent experience with break-ups. "Life goes on, right?" Steve added.

"That's what they say."

"She was a good lady," Steve said. "I know you'll miss her a lot. But you know what? There are plenty of good ladies out there. You'll find another before you know it."

The problem was, Scott had already found another. Kerry. Only he'd found her too soon, when neither of them had been ready for each other. Now that maybe they were—now that he was ready, at least—she was MIA, somewhere down in the swamps with Mother Blessing. Out of touch, but not out of mind.

He hoped she would contact him over the holidays, because he was turning over an idea in his mind, persuading himself to commit to it, and it would involve her. At least, after the fact.

He couldn't say anything about that to Steve, however, or tell his brother how much he hoped she was okay. He hated the fact that he was unable to reach her—he could send e-mails to her address, which she could sometimes log on and receive through some magical Internet access Mother Blessing had arranged. But there were no guarantees that she'd get them, and he couldn't call her, and he had no way of knowing for certain that she was safe down there.

"You're right," he said after a while. "Brandy's great, but there'll be others. Like Linda, right?"

"Exactly," Steve agreed. "Just like that. Give it some time, that's all I'm saying."

"I hear you." Scott nodded and glanced toward the screen, where Indiana Jones was in mortal danger yet again. Somehow he always pulled out of it. Like Kerry, he was gutsy and resourceful. Like Indy, Kerry had always managed to survive.

So far.

Scott only hoped that if there ever came a time when she needed him to help her do so, he would be there for her.

New York at Thanksgiving was a magical city. The usual bustle went on, but people's moods seemed improved somehow—strangers smiled at one another on the sidewalks instead of growling. Horns still honked, but the blasts were shorter, not as angry. Rebecca Levine was willing to admit that it might simply have been her imagination, that because she loved the holiday season she projected that feeling on those she saw.

But she had grown accustomed to the Santa Cruz lifestyle; the small California beach town felt like home to her now. She had grown up in the city, in her family's Upper West Side apartment. Her room was still there, and it was still home in a way, but the city felt alien now, crowded and impersonal. It was only at this time of year, between Thanksgiving and New Year's Eve, that she really enjoyed being back.

She had stayed in yesterday, watching the Macy's parade on TV but unwilling to brave the crowds to see it in person. Today she ventured out into the wind and cold, partly just to see the city in her favorite dressing, and partly to get away from her family. Her father had taken a few days off from his insurance company job to spend time with her, since she was out from California. Her mother only worked part-time, and little sister Miriam was off from high school for a week. So privacy was hard to come by in the apartment, and after sharing a comparatively large house with just Erin, Rebecca had become accustomed to plenty of privacy.

Plus, people kept trying to cheer her up.

That was probably okay, probably what families were supposed to do. Miriam, especially, was relentless, regaling Rebecca nonstop with stories about who was going out with whom, and who had said what, and what did people think about this, until Rebecca thought she was about to explode.

Because the world wasn't about which girl liked what boy who didn't like her back. At least Rebecca's wasn't.

In Rebecca's world, Season Howe existed. Witchcraft was real—and terrifyingly deadly. Friends died. Witches could use stupid college kid séances to hunt people down.

There was a lot in life to be thankful for, but having the blinders ripped off, being exposed to the truth about the supernatural world that paralleled the one most people thought of as real, wasn't part of that.

Rebecca would rather have lived in blissful ignorance of the whole thing. But that ignorance had been torn away from her, and there was no going back. It meant building walls between herself and her family, because there were so many things she couldn't talk to them about. Every conversation had to be parsed to make sure she didn't accidentally say something about Mother Blessing, or Josh's brutal murder, or Season.

So getting away from the apartment, losing herself in the happy holiday crowds, was her answer. At least short-term.

Rebecca had a few more weeks of school before the long winter break, which meant she'd have to go back to Santa Cruz. She found that the prospect pleased her.

In Santa Cruz she'd be alone. But at least she wouldn't be alone in the midst of her whole family.

She thought maybe that was better.

Kerry Profitt's diary, November 26.
Never let it be said that a night's sleep can't do a world of good.

Okay, to be completely accurate, more than a night. I crashed almost as soon as I got into the Hendersons' car—and a good thing for me they were basically honest folks, right?—and didn't wake up until we were in Portsmouth. Then once they shook me into consciousness, they drove around until they found a hotel that they were comfortable letting me stay in. Never mind that they still didn't know the first thing about me, except maybe that I snored and drooled a little (okay, maybe not, but who knows? It's not like I was awake and watching). Never mind, too, that I'd have been satisfied at that point with a cot and a soft rock for a pillow.

But the place they found was clean and tidy, with locks on the doors and starched sheets and everything. I checked in, paid in advance with cash, went up to my ninth-floor room. Once I got there, I realized that I was ravenous.

So guess what: room service!

No greens or pork chops or Scooter Pies or any of that stuff that Mother Blessing lives on, either. I ordered a steak, medium-rare, with fries, a salad, and a slice of cheesecake. Ate every bite. Then I took a bath that lasted more than an hour, running more hot water every time it turned too cool. When I started to get so sleepy I worried about drowning, I got out, toweled off, and climbed in between the crisp white sheets.

That must have been about six. In the P.M.

When I woke up again it was past noon. Princess Aurora, much?

Now I'm sitting on the queen-size bed, the big TV with cable channels and everything running to give me some company, typing this on the trusty laptop that, miraculously, survived my escape from the swamp. Outside the floor-to-ceiling windows, the sun is setting, the sky over the Atlantic is purple and indigo with a few streaks of salmon. There's a sandwich on the way up, courtesy of room service again— well, I guess it's not courtesy if you pay for it, right? But still . . .

Still, the point is that now I'm awake and fed and there's a laundry room in the building, so soon I'll have clean clothes, and downstairs there's one of those little overpriced hotel shops, so I have makeup—real makeup, for the first time in months! So . . .

. . . it's time to figure out what's next.

And that, dear diary, is the hard part.

I got away from Mother Blessing. For now, at least, which is not to say that she won't send someone—or something—after me still. She's kind of run out of sons, but she still can manufacture simulacra to hunt for her.

Not that I'm as big a problem for her as Season is. But I get the feeling she was a little ticked off that I ran out on her like that. And I get the additional— and related—feeling that she is a sore loser. So I've got to watch my step, Mother Blessing—wise.

And the other thing is that Season is still out

there in the great wide world someplace. She is still, whatever the real story between her and Mother Blessing, the person who killed Daniel. And Mace and Josh. She's got a lot to answer for.

I've got a few new tricks up my metaphorical sleeve that I didn't have before, thanks to Mother Blessing (I keep wanting to write Mama B., but somehow, even though I know she'll never read this diary, I can't quite bring myself to do it). I know enough to get myself out of a swamp that wants to keep me there. What I don't know, I'm pretty certain, is enough to be much more than a momentary headache for Season Howe. I definitely am not skilled enough to defeat her in one-on-one combat, unless maybe she was comatose. And tied up.

Even then it wouldn't be a given.

So my quandary—and isn't that a great word, quandary?—is, how do I hone my skills now? How do I learn more, so that I can go after Season with some hope of winning? Who is there to teach me all the things I don't know?

I can't beat Season. But I can't really rest until Season is beaten. I can't beat Mother Blessing, but I can't give up until I know what really happened in Slocumb, and whether Mother Blessing, as I'm coming to believe, bears a lot more responsibility for what happened to Daniel than I originally thought.

Hence, quandary. Dilemma. Perplexity, even.

Hark—a knock at the door. Room service.

More later.

K.

3

Kerry stayed in the Portsmouth hotel for two more nights, watching the world from the ninth floor, behind the protection of a deadbolt lock. The TV stayed on most of that time as Kerry caught up on the various news items, reality shows, sitcoms, and personal hygiene commercials she had missed during her time in the swamp. All in all, she decided, she really hadn't missed much of any importance at all.

But on the last night she started to feel uneasy. This was far too close to Mother Blessing for any kind of real comfort. And she didn't have any fake ID, so she had checked in under her own name. It wouldn't take much effort to find her here.

If anyone was looking. That was the big

question mark, the great unknown. She had every reason to suspect that Season might be— she had, after all, shown up at Rebecca's séance and then found Josh in Las Vegas.

Or was it Josh who found her? That part was never completely clear. If that was the case, then maybe the séance sighting was the optical illusion Rebecca had first thought it was. Maybe Season wasn't hunting them after all.

Which would be good, because it would take some of the heat off Kerry while she figured out how to go about hunting Season herself.

Her first priority had to be getting out of this neighborhood. Where to go, she hadn't yet determined. She didn't think she had to cover her tracks as much as she had when she had run away from Northwestern to come down here. Then, she had worried that her Aunt Betty and Uncle Marsh would call the cops when they learned she was missing, and she needed to make sure she couldn't be easily found. She knew Mother Blessing would have her own methods of searching for her, but she highly doubted that involving the authorities would be one of them.

When she woke up the next morning, she had the answer.

Hide in plain sight, she thought. She would go home—back to Illinois, back to Aunt Betty and Uncle Marsh. Then even if there was any kind of search effort going on, it would be called off. Mother Blessing would never think she would go back there, so it would be the last place she'd look. The other alternative was going back to Northwestern, but she was pretty sure she'd have been expelled by now, what with the not going to class or making her tuition payments.

She called for room service one last time, showered, ate breakfast. When she was done with that, she packed her duffel again and caught a hotel shuttle to the airport. There was a flight to Chicago that afternoon that she could get on, and then a commuter plane down to Cairo. Still weary, she dozed on the longer flight, but on the commuter she stayed awake, drinking bottled water and paging through a magazine.

From the airport she took a taxi. At nine-thirty, she knocked on the door of her aunt and uncle's home, a single-story ranch house with snow on the front lawn and the blue glow of a TV showing in a window.

Uncle Marsh opened the door with a half-empty highball glass in his hand and a questioning look in his eyes. He stood unsteadily in the doorway for a moment, as if unsure of what he was seeing.

"Hi, Uncle Marsh," Kerry said meekly.

He put an arm around her shoulders and drew her into the house. His breath reeked of alcohol. "Call off the Coast Guard, Betty!" he called. "Look what the cat dragged in!"

Aunt Betty emerged from the kitchen carrying a dishtowel and a china plate, which dropped from her hand the instant she saw Kerry standing in the entryway. It hit the ground and smashed into a hundred pieces. "Kerry!" she cried, and ran toward her niece.

Standing there, enveloped by her closest living relatives, Kerry had a moment of wondering why she had ever left this house. But that only lasted for a few moments. Aunt Betty was weeping openly and clinging to her, repeating, "We were so worried about you," over and over. Uncle Marsh knuckled Kerry lightly on the chin and said, "I was just joking about the Coast Guard. We figured if you'd wanted us to know where you were, you'd have told us."

And then it all came flooding back. Uncle Marsh was a drunk, a harsh man who had taken every tenderness ever offered him and turned it away, using a crude sense of humor like a shield against the blades of kindness. Aunt Betty gave new meaning to the term codependent, and the worse Uncle Marsh behaved toward her—or anyone else, for that matter, within earshot of her—the more she decided he needed to be protected. From what, Kerry was never really sure. But she became his one-woman security squad, running interference, keeping him safe from his own worst instincts. She wept openly and often, which drove him mad. The madder he got, the more she decided that he was being persecuted, and the more she wept.

Kerry hadn't been inside for ten minutes before she realized that coming back here was one of the biggest mistakes she had ever made. She would have been better off letting them think she was dead. At least then they could have continued driving each other crazy without dragging her back into it.

The next morning she sat at the table having breakfast with Aunt Betty. Uncle Marsh was still asleep—sleeping off the effects of the previous night's alcohol intake, Kerry guessed, although Aunt Betty insisted that he had been "working awfully hard lately." Kerry had managed to forestall the inquisition last night by claiming exhaustion, but she knew it couldn't be dodged forever.

"I called the police last night and told them to stop looking for you, Kerry," Aunt Betty said over the rim of a bone china teacup. She was a birdlike woman, thin and frail, with bad eyes for which she wore glasses whose lenses were nearly as big as her entire head, a pointed beak of a nose protruding from between them. Her hair was brown, but from a bottle, because it should have been gray years before. She held her cup in two bony hands. "We really were terribly worried about you when you just disappeared. The college called, and that girl you shared a room with, Sophia—"

"Sonya," Kerry corrected. She pushed

runny scrambled eggs around on her plate with her fork. There were many ways to describe Aunt Betty, but "skilled chef" would never be one of them.

"Right, Sonya. She was no help at all. She said you were antisocial—which Marsh and I, of course, knew wasn't true—and that you had probably gone to live in a cave somewhere. Well, I said that was just the most ridiculous thing I had ever heard, that my niece wasn't the kind of girl who would live in a cave, and that you were perfectly nice and very reliable, and if you were gone, then obviously something had happened to you. You were kidnapped, or murdered, or something like that."

"Well, I'm fine," Kerry said. She bit into some rubbery bacon.

"I can see that, and I'm so glad to hear it. I told the police that, of course, after I saw you. The detective who's had your case, a young man, Pembroke or something like that, he called back first thing this morning while you were sleeping, and said that he'll be by this afternoon to talk to you. He'd like to know where you've been, of course, and he'd like to know whatever happened to you.

"We all would like to know that, of course. I'm sure it was something just dreadful."

She continued yammering on, speaking words that Kerry was no longer listening to, without seeming to notice that Kerry hadn't replied. What could she tell the police? "Sorry, detective, but I was off learning magic so I can kill the witch who killed my boyfriend. Next time, I'll call more often."

Yeah, that'll fly.

She had managed to convince herself that Uncle Marsh and Aunt Betty would be glad she had disappeared. They no longer bore any financial burden on her behalf, if they ever had—an insurance settlement, after her mother's death, had paid for Kerry's college, and even though there wasn't much of an estate left after all her mom's medical bills, the sale of the house they had lived in had netted some money for her aunt and uncle.

And Uncle Marsh had wasted no time—as soon as she left for school, not even waiting for her to vanish completely—in turning "her" room back into the den it had been before she had come to live in their house. She had spent the night on a foldaway couch in there, with

Marsh's big-screen TV and wet bar. She always thought their house looked like something decorated from a thrift store, except that the reverse was true: Their furnishings were the kind that ended up at thrift stores, but they were the original owners. There were lots of items that looked like carefully tooled wood, except that they were really molded wood-grain plastic, lots of veneers, lots of composition board. Everything except real wood, it seemed.

Given her uncle's speed at eliminating every trace of Kerry from the house, the fact that they'd called the police at all was a little staggering. The idea that she would have to explain her whereabouts to the authorities was terrifying. How thoroughly would they check her story out, if at all? If she claimed to have run away to San Francisco, or Sweden, would they ask for addresses? Known associates? Would they expect some kind of verification of her statement? If she turned out to simply be a runaway, instead of a kidnap victim, would they want to be repaid for the expense of their investigation?

She doubted that, but on the rest of it she

was completely in the dark. She hadn't anticipated anything like this when she came back here.

"Aunt Betty," she said, interrupting whatever her aunt was going on about now. "I'm not sure I'm really . . . you know, up to talking to the police today. Can't we just tell them that I'm fine, and let it go at that? I mean, don't they have better things to do than investigate people who aren't missing anymore?"

"Well, but they'll want to try to find whoever took you," Aunt Betty said.

"No one took me, Aunt Betty. I . . . had something I needed to do. I went to where I could do it. I . . . well, I didn't do it all, not really. Not yet. But I did some of it, and then I came back."

Aunt Betty regarded her, the teacup cradled in both hands again like something rare and precious. "You just . . . left?"

"I'm almost eighteen, Aunt Betty. I'm capable of making my own decisions. It was something very important."

"It must have been," the older woman said. "Aren't you going to tell me what it was?"

Kerry looked at her plate. "I can't."

"I see." A long pause, and then the teacup clattered in its saucer. Aunt Betty's hands were trembling, and when Kerry looked up, she saw tears welling in her aunt's eyes. "Noreen trusted us," she said. She almost never used her sister's name, it was always "your mother." "I'm sorry you can't."

"It isn't that, Aunt Betty," Kerry said, already knowing the conversation had veered from difficult to hopeless. "It's just . . . it's hard to explain. I can't explain. Not without telling you . . . telling you everything. And I can't do that. I guess I'm asking you to trust me, this time."

"I see." Again with that. She always said that when, of course, she didn't see—when she couldn't see at all. Soon the tears would be flowing, and the sacrifices they had made would be drawn into the discussion—sacrifices which were real, Kerry had no doubt about that. She appreciated completely the fact that they had opened their house to a child who was not their daughter, whom they had never asked for.

"I'm so sorry, Aunt Betty," Kerry said, hoping to head all that off at the pass. "I really . . .

I wish it hadn't happened the way it did. I wish I could tell you the whole story. I honestly do. But . . . it's something you're better off not knowing, you've got to believe that."

"Yes, well . . ." Tears ran down Aunt Betty's cheeks now, and she dabbed at them with a paper napkin. At least she hadn't started sobbing. That was the worst.

"Haven't you ever known something you wish you didn't, Aunt Betty?" Kerry pressed. She blinked, feeling tears of her own coming on now. "Something that you couldn't tell another soul about, something that was just too huge and too terrible to share? That's what I have, what I know. I can't tell you what it is, and you wouldn't believe me, probably, if I did. And if by some miracle I could convince you, it still wouldn't do you any good to know it. It would only make you miserable, in fact. So why share it? Why work so hard to persuade you of something that you can't do anything about and that will only make you hurt? I can't do it to you and Uncle Marsh. I'm sorry that it's this way, but it is. There's nothing I can do about that now. No way I can undo it. The best I can do is try to make it right, and even if I do that, you'll never know about it. . . . But I will.

"So that's what I have to try to do. And you—you'll just have to try to understand that I love you, and you'll have to either trust me, or—or not trust me, I guess. I hope it's trust, but it really doesn't make much difference, either way, in the long run."

Kerry snatched her napkin from her lap and blew her nose. Aunt Betty was sobbing now, long looping sobs that Kerry had always thought must have been a real hit at funerals. And Kerry was crying too, tears falling from her cheeks and splashing into the watery eggs and rubbery bacon she hadn't eaten. Tears that came from knowing that she had somehow stepped off the path her life was supposed to have taken onto a different one, a road that was dark and frightening, for which there was no map and no guide. Tears for her mother, who couldn't be around to try to deal with this new and sinister aspect of her life, and tears for her aunt, who was but could never understand it. Tears, too, for Daniel, whom she had known for so short a span and loved so hard, who had both set her on this path and tried to protect her from it.

Both women cried now, sitting at the breakfast table, each consumed by her own private grief that Kerry suspected had little, if anything, to do with the other's.

Which was when Uncle Marsh wandered in, unshaven, his white hair askew, in a sleeveless white T-shirt and flannel pajama bottoms, scratching his belly under the shirt.

"Who died?" he asked.

And Kerry started to laugh through her tears.

4

Kerry hadn't unpacked her bag yet, so it didn't take her long to get ready to move on again. Aunt Betty called the police detective she had been talking to and told him that the whole affair had been a misunderstanding, that Kerry had left school of her own free will and now was back. The detective peppered her with questions for a few minutes, but agreed to close the books on the case. Kerry was still a little surprised that there had been a case with open books in the first place.

She found herself oddly touched by it, and by Aunt Betty's willingness to help. Uncle Marsh remained his typical grumpy self, and Kerry tried to limit her interaction with him to just the right amount so that she might actually miss him when she left.

Even though she had barely arrived, there was still a lot to get done. Aunt Betty drove her downtown to a branch of her bank, where she withdrew a few thousand more dollars from her insurance money to cover expenses wherever her new course took her. When they got back home, Aunt Betty suggested that Kerry take a look inside some boxes she had stored in the attic—things that had belonged to Kerry's parents, as well as some of Kerry's childhood items—while she made lunch.

The attic was close and musty, and even though the air outside was near freezing, Kerry found it uncomfortably warm up there. Aunt Betty had separated out the boxes that had come from Kerry's parents' house, so Kerry knew just which ones to look at. Each box was taped across the top. Kerry took a knife up with her and sliced through the tape carefully so she wouldn't damage any of the contents.

She had no memory of this stuff being packed up, even though she must have been around. Her mother's death had been hard on her, but in a way—after nursing her through illness for more than a year, alone because her father had died a couple of years before that—it had been both a heartbreak and a relief. Her mother's long suffering had finally come to an end, and Kerry, having been pressed into service at too young an age, could have what was left of her teen years.

Well, we know how that worked out, Kerry thought grimly. Her first summer out of high school had been spent in San Diego for a summer resort job. That had ended when Daniel Blessing had stumbled, injured, into her life, and she and her housemates had been swept up into his world—a world of dangerous witchcraft and intrigue.

Not so much the teenage dream, she knew. It was okay, though. She had learned long ago that adaptability was one of her strong points—a key to survival, really. *Go where the river takes you.*

But during that period, right after her mother's death, she had been an emotional basket case, she remembered. Aunt Betty and Uncle Marsh had packed up the house and sold most of the furnishings and the property. They had been named Kerry's guardians and the executors of her mom's will. Which made it not especially shocking that she would have been unaware of precisely what had been saved and stored up here.

Some of the things she found were expected, but they still brought a lump to her throat. Her parents' wedding album and a couple of additional albums of family photos, including shots of Kerry as a little girl, dark haired, wide eyed, and skinny. Her dad had called her string bean until she was twelve, when she declared that he was never to use that term around her again. Old documents: tax information, birth and death certificates, medical records. A few objects that probably could have been sold or that Aunt Betty herself could have used—some jewelry, an antique music box with intricate gold filigree, a set of fine silverware that had been a wedding present from Kerry's grandmother and that had always remained inside its cherrywood box, "for company."

Then there were the boxes that had come from Kerry's room, where less stuff had been disposed of. Kerry found old school papers, mostly forgotten, including some that made her smile with fond memories of certain teachers and friends. Books she'd liked over the years, going back to *Where the Wild Things Are* and Dr. Seuss, all the way up through her poetry phase in high school, including such diverse poets as Sylvia Plath, Robert Frost, Walt Whitman, and Pablo Neruda. A small selection of mysteries, including Nancy Drews and Agatha Christies. Mostly, after about the sixth grade, she had read books from school libraries or Cairo's public library system and from her parents' library, so her own collection was limited. But she found herself glad that Aunt Betty had saved these, and she hoped that one of these days she'd be able to settle in one place so that she could have them again.

She found old toys, locked diaries, drawings she had made, yearbooks friends had signed for her. Nothing earth-shattering, but looking through the boxes somehow crystallized things for her. Her life had been one thing, now it was another. The past was part of her; there was no denying its influence. But it didn't define her by itself, and it didn't control her direction from here. She found that she could remember it with a sense of pleasant nostalgia without feeling that she had to be dragged back into the life she had left behind.

Her life, Kerry decided, was like these boxes. The part of it that was her childhood, that included her parents, could be wrapped up in paper and sealed inside one box. It would never change; it was what it was. The precious part spent with Daniel could go into a second box. The third box had to remain open—it included everything since Daniel's death, and it was an unfinished project. There would come a time, she believed, when it could be wrapped and stored as well, but she didn't know what the shape of it would be at that time.

Whether she'd be alive to do the wrapping was anybody's guess.

Kerry spent one more night under Aunt Betty and Uncle Marsh's roof. The next day they drove her to the airport. Aunt Betty welled up again; Uncle Marsh was gruff and offhand about the whole thing. Kerry figured he was just glad to get his house back, while Aunt Betty had seen her as a kind of reinforcement in her ongoing struggle with his drinking, his temper, and his generally unpleasant attitude. But she would never leave him, Kerry knew, never even force the issue of him changing his ways, because the worse he got the more she protected him from himself and others.

As she walked through the terminal, past the point where only ticketed passengers could go, she found herself glad for the short time she had spent with them—happy she had been able to spend it, but also happy that it had been so brief. She had an hour to wait for her flight, so she sat in the waiting area and studied every blond head she saw, just in case one might be Season. Not seeing her, she took one of Daniel's journals from her duffel and started to flip through it, looking for a section she hadn't read yet.

> There comes a time in the life of every young man when he must leave the home of his parents and make his own way in the world, for good or ill. In my case, this time was doubly complicated. First, I have a twin, Abraham, so there are two of us, not one, striking out to find our fortunes. And second, our father has been gone for our entire life, so when we left, that meant Mother Blessing would truly be alone for the first time in a very long while.

Perhaps triply complicated would be more apt, for there was yet another matter to consider. We were not leaving simply to start families and households of our own. We were leaving with a very particular purpose in mind—one that has been instilled in us from our earliest days.

Mother Blessing had trained us and instructed us. We were ready, we were equipped, and we were anxious to go forth into the world to find and destroy Season Howe. As we have learned since infancy, she killed our father, demolished our town, and drove our mother into hiding in the swamp. Mother Blessing alone knows the truth of that day, so long ago in Slocumb, and Season will likely not rest until she has murdered the last surviving witness of her crime. Abe and I are to locate her and make sure she can never accomplish that sordid goal.

Though Season has had years to hide herself away, we are not without clues. There is, in the community of witchcraft, some small amount of communication. Season has been seen, and spoken to, here and there. Reports of her whereabouts occasionally reach Mother Blessing. A pattern has been observed.

Season Howe, unlike Mother Blessing, does not confine herself to a specific location. She moves from place to place, occupying new homes like a hermit crab inhabiting the shell of some other creature. She seems to make few alliances, and those temporary and short-lived. She wants for little, and seems always to have means at her disposal. Though it is unusual for a woman to travel alone, she does so often, and not just within the colonies but also to foreign lands.

Our most recent report, although it was several months old by the time word reached Mother Blessing in the swamp, had her in the city of Providence, in Rhode Island. Abe and I packed a trunk, loaded it into a wagon, and set off, striving for manly composure in the face of Mother Blessing's weeping. She had known that we must depart, of course, for it was she who set us on our path, she who taught us from childhood what our task in life must be. Even so, the actual doing of it, setting out on that journey, was a sorrowful event for us all, as it must always be.

And yet our circumstance is not like that of others, as Abe and I discussed on the road today. Other men of our age are indeed setting out to build their own lives. But we are different, we know. We have every expectation of living far longer than they. In a very few years they will be twenty, their lives likely half over already. When we reach twenty our lives will still be in the beginning stages, still in relative infancy. We will likely still not have achieved the full measure of our powers, but at some point thereafter our aging will cease, or at least slow considerably. Time, which has passed for us at much the same pace as it has for other boys, will, from this point forward, mean something very different. The days will pass, but each one will be the merest moment in time for us, each year as an hour or less.

Abraham and I know this to be true, and yet we struggle with the idea. We are not immortal, but we are witch born and *witch bred, and so as close to that exalted state as mortal man can be.*

Our journey is just begun. We may find Season at its end, and we may not. But if she eludes us now, we will have time enough to seek her out again.

We will, in fact, have all the time in the world.

I remain, Daniel Blessing. Ninth of August, 1720.

Her flight called, Kerry wrapped the leather thong around the book and tied it. He had been just sixteen when he wrote that, she realized. Younger than she was now—a boy, by contemporary standards. But that was a different world—she would have been considered an old maid, unmarried a week before her eighteenth birthday. If all this had been revealed to her at sixteen, she was sure, she would have fallen apart, completely unable to handle it. She supposed she had been relatively mature for her age, since she was effectively running a household and helping to care for a mother who could barely get out of bed. But there was a big difference between that and being willing to accept evidence of witchcraft, of magical feuds that had been raging for longer than there had been a United States.

All in all she thought she had handled it pretty well. And continued to do so. Like Daniel in his journal entry, she was leaving home—or the place that had once been her home, if only briefly—with no certainty of when, or if, she would return. The last time she had gone away she had done it in secret, but this time her aunt and uncle knew where she was going, if not why. Last time she had been consumed with a specific desire: to find Mother Blessing and learn magic. This time her goal was more vague. She wanted to find Season, but didn't know where to look. She did know, however, that she didn't want to make Cairo her base of operations—she couldn't bring herself to live in Aunt Betty and Uncle Marsh's home again and didn't want to expose them to possible danger even if she could.

A few minutes later, Kerry was buckled into her seat and a flight attendant was demonstrating how oxygen masks would fall from above in the event of a sudden loss of cabin pressure. As the plane headed down the runway, a sense of ease fell over her. With no specific urgency before her, no crisis under way, she was more relaxed and comfortable than she had been in a long time.

She hoped the feeling would last a while.

5

Their friend and was…

Kerry flew into San Jose, and Rebecca Levine met her at the airport. She hadn't seen Rebecca since Las Vegas, when Josh had died. They had talked a couple of times since then, most recently when she had called from Aunt Betty's to tell Rebecca she was headed for California. But they hadn't spent any real time together since summer, in San Diego, before the group had split up to go their separate ways.

When she came out of the gate, Rebecca ran to her with a squeal, embracing her like a long-lost sister. "Kerry!" she shrieked. "Oh my God, it's so good to see you!"

"Hey, Beck," Kerry replied, a little more subdued. "It's great to see you too."

"We have so much to talk about," Rebecca gushed. Kerry thought her enthusiasm sounded a little forced, and when she pulled away from the hug she realized that Rebecca had lost weight, probably twenty pounds or so. Her typically loose clothing—in blues and golds today, a pleated long skirt with striped tights under it and a voluminous fuzzy sweater—hung on her, and there were dark circles under her eyes. A red paisley bandanna covered copper hair that looked like it could use some attention. Rebecca hadn't complained of any problems on the phone, but it was obvious at a glance that something was very wrong.

"I guess we do," Kerry agreed. She had carried on her one bag, so they walked straight outside to Rebecca's parked car. It was dark out, and cool, but not nearly as cold as Illinois had been. As they walked, Rebecca babbled casually about classes, her roommate Erin, and life in Santa Cruz.

It wasn't until they were on the freeway, heading south over the coastal hills, that she stopped her constant, upbeat chatter. She glanced over at Kerry. "I'm . . . uh . . . I'm not doing so well," she admitted.

"I kinda guessed that," Kerry said.

"Yeah, I know. I'm a mess."

"That's overstating it," Kerry answered. "But I've seen you looking better."

"Yeah," Rebecca said again. She returned her attention to the freeway, driving with both hands firmly on the wheel. "I don't know exactly what it is. I went home for Thanksgiving, but I just couldn't wait to get back here, you know? I wanted to be here. Dad said I was becoming a hermit and I needed to snap out of it. He's probably right, but he let me come anyway."

"You said you had only been back for a day when I called," Kerry remembered. "How was New York?"

"I don't know. I love New York at this time of year. I thought it would snap me out of this . . . this funk that I've been in. But instead it just got worse. It's like, when there are that many people on the streets, and a significant percentage of them have their heads covered, you can't even tell which ones are blond. Any of them could be Season. I thought I saw her a few days ago when I went down to Ground Zero, and I screamed. People looked at me like I was freaking insane. I guess maybe I am."

Kerry had known it wouldn't be long until Season's name came up. She was the great uniter, the common bond that held their summer group together long after they would ordinarily have lost touch. "I don't think you're crazy, Beck," she said, stroking Rebecca's arm. "Season is a scary person. You saw her, or thought you did, and then she killed Josh. And then—you don't know this yet, so don't let it freak you out more, because I'm here and okay—she came to the swamp. Mother Blessing and I fought her."

Rebecca almost lost control of the car, swerving into another lane, and a horn blasted behind them. "Oh, jeez, I'm sorry!" she said after she had corrected her course. "Kerry, are you okay? What happened?"

Kerry told her about the assault on Mother Blessing's cabin, and about the things Season had said—and implied. She explained her suspicions—that Mother Blessing seemed to know an awful lot about the destruction of Slocumb for someone who claimed to have run away to hide in the swamp; that she had apparently kept from her sons, and from everyone else, the fact that Season was her own mother;

that she had tried to keep Kerry in the swamp by force when she'd started to run away.

"I don't know anything for certain, really," she admitted after she had detailed the whole story. "And I'm sure if we asked her, Mother Blessing would have all kinds of excuses and explanations. But I just get a bad vibe from her—and I've come to trust feelings like that, intuitions, vibrations, a lot more since I started learning witchcraft. There's more to them than we sometimes think."

"Seems like there's more to lots of things," Rebecca agreed. She paid attention to the road as they came down a long slope, with the lights of Santa Cruz spreading before them. "There's home," she announced.

"It looks nice," Kerry said. The town hugged the shore—she could see moonlight sparkling on the water. The city was not big, but a small, comfortable size.

"It's great," Rebecca said. "When it's daylight I'll show you the boardwalk and the beach and all that good stuff. It still feels like an old-time California beach town."

"That's cool." But Kerry couldn't help thinking that an old-time California beach town would be full of blondes. She was worried about Rebecca, concerned that her friend was letting her fear of Season develop into full-blown paranoia. While she was here, she'd have to focus on helping Rebecca get better—sleeping and eating on a regular schedule, going to school, and not worrying too much about things she couldn't control.

She glanced at Rebecca, driving with one hand now while she nibbled on the fingernails of the other.

This might be a lot of work, she thought.

Kerry Profitt's diary, December 16.

Beethoven's birthday. At least, according to the old Peanuts cartoons. I haven't run across any specific references in Daniel's journals, but Beethoven lived and died during his lifetime, so I suppose it's possible they crossed paths at some point. It always strikes me as weird that someone I knew was alive at the same time as people who I think of as practically pre-historic.

Santa Cruz is a pretty awesome little town. It doesn't have the natural beauty that La Jolla did, but it's more laid back, less glitzily commercial than La

Jolla. Rebecca was right, now that I have spent some time here—it does have a kind of old-fashioned charm to it. The boardwalk has carnival games and a roller coaster (that you'll never catch me on), and the beach is full of surfers in wet suits. Of course, it's winter—probably in summer it's also full of sun worshippers and families.

Near the beach is a railroad trestle that looks sort of like the one in Stand by Me, except for the lack of adolescents about to get run over by a train. Plenty of adolescents hanging around it, though, and jumping from it for kicks.

Not me. I'm sitting on the rocks nearby, watching them as I write in my too-long-neglected journal. The day is cold, with a brisk wind coming in off the water, making me glad I'm not trying to write the old-fashioned way. The laptop screen doesn't blow around like notebook paper would. I'm bundled up in a watch cap and coat and jeans and my red-checked tennies with thick white socks, and anyway, as a Midwestern girl I'm still used to real winters, not this kind, so I am not overly concerned.

Except, of course, about Rebecca.

I don't think she sleeps for more than three hours at a stretch, ever. I've been staying at her house for a while now, crashing on the living room sofa, and I hear her at all hours. She says she's going to sleep, but then I wake up and she's reading, or she's online, or she's sipping hot chocolate by her window, looking out at an empty street.

As if she's afraid someone will be out there.

Which, duh. She is.

I have tried to tell her she's safe with me here. I've done a couple of little demonstrations, some handy tricks I picked up back in the swamp. But she knows I still am not nearly powerful enough to beat Season, if she decided to come around.

And maybe it's worse with me here. Maybe, since I've seen Season more recently than she has—and since Mother Blessing is a little miffed at me too—she's afraid that my presence here makes this place even more likely to be visited sometime. She could be right. That's the thing. None of us know Season's mind, or Mother Blessing's for that matter.

For the first week or so I thought she was doing better. I got her eating regular meals, even though it meant getting up early enough to cook her some breakfast before her first class. I woke her up, walked her to campus, hung out there or went downtown while she was in class. Met her in the afternoon and came back here with her. She had a job earlier in the fall, but apparently she just stopped going.

Usually a good way to become "formerly employed."

Then it was my eighteenth birthday, and she wanted to have a big celebration. Planned it out. She would invite a bunch of people, have snacks, drinks, music. She talked about it for days. December 9 came, and hey, I'm legally an adult for most purposes. I can vote, I can join the army, I can do lots of things.

What I couldn't do was get Rebecca out of bed.

Missed her first class. Halfway through what would have been her second, she finally emerged. Puffy-eyed, teary. "I'm canceling the party," she said. "I can't do it. I haven't been able to go to a party since that night."

Now, the party? Not really that big a deal to me. Turning 18 is cool and I'm glad I made it this far— and, as an aside, I totally loved the pen she bought me, silver and chunky, with purple trim and a clip so I can hang it on my backpack or whatever, so happy birthday to me—but I don't need a bunch of strangers to validate that. What bothered me was, she wanted to cancel it because months ago she went to a party at which there was a séance, and at that séance she thought maybe this blond chick turned into Season Howe for a second.

And okay, it freaked her out. Can't blame her for that.

But is she going to let that one incident rule her life? I mean, we all watched Season kill Daniel in front of a house, but that hasn't kept her out of houses. We know Mace was killed by his car, or in it, and ditto for cars.

Me? Never so much the party girl to begin with. But I wouldn't let one Season sighting keep me away from them forever, especially if they were something I liked in the first place.

I've spent the week since then trying to keep her steady, but it seems like she's getting worse, not better. Sleeping less. Eating when I sit down with her and watch her, but I don't think she eats a bite if I'm not right there. I hear her at night sometimes, crying, when she thinks I'm asleep.

Paging Doc Brandy. Rebecca has a serious problem here, and it's something I am not equipped to deal with, I guess. I mean, shaking her a lot and shouting, "Snap out of it, girl!" probably won't help, right?

Beyond that, I'm fresh out of ideas. And she's not going to have a very happy Hanukkah if I can't figure something out fast.

More later.

K.

In the run-up to the holidays, the ski resorts were full of people. New England was loaded with resorts, of course—winter sports were practically a religion here. But Scott guessed that New Hampshire's were the most prized, particularly those centered in the White Mountains. He seemed to spend most of his day in traffic, jammed between SUVs with skis and snowboards on their roof racks, loaded with folks in bright-colored outfits and dark tans.

These were his people, but they were not. He was of their social class and background, and had he chosen to be a ski bum or a 'boarder, he could have. But the whole thing just seemed too elite for his tastes—he couldn't enjoy an expensive hobby knowing that there were millions of people who couldn't afford a square meal, much less lift tickets and Rossignols. He knew it was a foolish attitude that marked him as a buzzkill to many people. He certainly wasn't opposed to fun, but there it was.

Still, he could afford the clothes and he had the car—okay, his SUV was just a RAV4, not a Hummer or anything, but it would pass. So he could move among his tribe as if he were a native. If only he could get through the traffic and find a parking space.

And the other problem was that there were so many resorts to choose from. His theory was that if, as Daniel had said, Season Howe liked to hide by moving from resort area to resort area, staying where populations were transient and most people didn't delve into the affairs of strangers, then in winter she'd be most likely to hang out at winter sports resorts. There was, of course, another alternative—that she might go to Florida or someplace warm for the winter, but he was just one guy and he couldn't be everywhere. The other alternative, worse yet, was that she would leave the country altogether.

That would just stink. Because Scott was determined to find her. School was out for a while, he had no girlfriend, no job, nothing to tie him to Cambridge or Boston. Sure, it'd be great if he could be home in time to spend Christmas with the family. But they'd just load him down with pricey gifts he couldn't really use and didn't want.

What he wanted was Season.

He thought he had developed something that resembled a plan. Nothing concrete, more of a feeling that might be worked into a real plan if he toyed with it. His idea was that Season's guard was probably up when there were other witches around, other magic users. Even in Las Vegas, when Josh was killed, Kerry had said she saw evidence of some of Mother Blessing's simulacra around.

So Scott reasoned that if there were no witches, no simulacra, no magic, maybe she would be more relaxed. If he could catch her with her defenses down, maybe a simple human-style killing would suffice.

So here he was, cruising the ski resorts of New Hampshire, with murder on his mind.

In Boston's combat zone, a guy with the money to spend could put his hands on just about anything he wanted to acquire. In this case what he had acquired, during one truly terrifying evening at some of the seediest bars he had ever imagined, was a Kel-Tec P11. It was a few years old, the guy said, a nine-mil with a ten-shot magazine and polymer grips. He barely knew what all that meant, just knew that the gun and a box of ammunition set him back a thousand bucks—and maybe ten years of his life, which he was pretty sure had run out of him in horrific sweat while he was making the buy. He was not a gun guy, and the idea of buying one and using it went against everything he had thought he stood for.

But he had seen Season. She might be a witch, but she was still a human being. A bullet could kill her.

All he had to do was find her.

He started at the aptly named Gunstock and worked his way north, through King Pine and Cranmore and then east into the White Mountains. Black Mountain, Attitash Bear Peak, the Waterville Valley. Which was where he was now, in the parking lot at the beautiful Golden Eagle Lodge, trying to angle into a parking spot that a full-sized Ford Expedition had just given up on. Scott was pretty sure he could slide the RAV4 into the space, though, if he could just get the right approach.

He waited for a couple of other vehicles to go past, and then he backed and filled until he made it in. He killed the ignition with a little flush of triumph and stepped outside into the blinding sun and snow.

Walking toward the Lodge, he was once again reminded that ski areas were crawling with blondes. He had to hope he could recognize Season if he saw her, and that she didn't recognize him. He didn't want to get into a confrontation with her—Brandy had always said he was an all-time champion at conflict avoidance, and she was usually right about that sort of thing. He just wanted to sneak up on her and drop her.

Him surviving was another big part of his almost-plan, because the deal was, once Season was down he would call Kerry at Rebecca's place, where, according to her latest e-mails, she had gone to stay. Part of the whole conflict-avoidance thing also meant that he was not exactly the big heroic type. But that didn't mean he never wanted to be, and if he could single-handedly off the big bad witch, that would be about as heroic as it got. Kerry could not fail to be impressed by that.

Even Brandy would take notice. But at this point Kerry's attention was more important to him. Brandy had hurt him, while Kerry had never really noticed him, romantically speaking—she was so hung up on Daniel she hadn't had eyes for anyone else. Now he could change that.

6

It was funny how one could see familiar places through fresh eyes, just by spending time with a new person. Adam Castle was a relative newcomer to Boston, having moved to the area just over a year before from Washington, D.C., to work on his master's degree at Harvard. But cities were his element, his passion, and he had delved into this one, quickly digging past its tourist facade and learning it like a native. He had taken Brandy to lunch at the Locke-Ober Café, an old-time, formal dining establishment where the waiters wore tuxedoes, even for lunch, and male guests were expected to wear jackets, and to one of the best dinners she'd ever had at Rialto, in the Charles Hotel in Harvard Square—a building she had seen a thousand times but had never thought to eat in.

Now he and Brandy walked hand in hand through the Quincy Market. In summer she liked to sit at the outdoor cafés and watch all the people, but this time of year, the indoors was much more comfortable. It was still crowded with tourists and locals alike, buying food at the market stalls or eating and drinking at the cafés. Musicians roamed the cobblestone promenade aisles and a juggler commanded a small crowd in one spot. A mime worked the masses too, but Brandy and Adam managed to dodge him.

People-watching had always been one of Brandy's favorite leisure-time pursuits. It fed her interest in psychology, her curiosity about the factors that make people act the way they do. Now everything had changed slightly. There was a new awareness that not everyone she saw was what they appeared to be from the outside—that some of them might, in fact, be more conversant with the supernatural than she'd have guessed. One couldn't go through experiences like she had, she theorized, without having those experiences color one's perceptions. People were still people, but her impressions of them had changed, as if she were eyeing them through a window glazed with ice, so reality shifted a fraction of an inch to the side.

"How did you like San Diego?" Adam asked her, once he had filled her with more information about Quincy Market than she had ever known.

"It was beautiful," she answered without even thinking about it. "The weather was just gorgeous. You know what they say, America's Finest City."

"That's what they say," Adam agreed. "But that's in terms of climate only. There are plenty of cities that beat it on almost every other score. For charm and natural beauty, San Francisco has it all over San Diego. For architectural beauty, Chicago. For sheer scale, of course, New York is the champ. San Diego has no history, especially if you compare it with Philadelphia or right here in Boston. In terms of being livable, its infrastructure is nothing compared to D.C., or New York, or Boston— there's no worthwhile public transportation there, and it's hard to get from one spot to another."

"Sounds like you've spent some time there," Brandy observed.

"Just a weekend," Adam admitted. "But I pack a lot into a weekend, and I've studied it."

"Maybe you should give it another try, and just spend a few days relaxing on the beach."

Adam shrugged. They stopped to look at a market stall selling oysters and every kind of lobster imaginable, from live ones to magnets, postcards, stuffed animals, and ceramic figures. "I will one of these days, I'm sure," he said. "But there are plenty of other places I'd like to see first."

"I hope you get to them all," she said. She was starting to hope she'd see some of them with him. This was their ninth date in two weeks, and she had already started thinking of him as her boyfriend. He made her laugh, he taught her things, and he had an easy self-confidence that made her comfortable right from the beginning. It had been a long time since she'd dated a black man, not for any special reason except that she wanted to live a color-blind life, in which the shade of one's skin was less important than the hue of the heart. His color made no difference to her now, either—it was his personality that was important, and the fact that, unlike Scott, he seemed to be with her because he wanted to be, not because the person he really wanted was unavailable.

Perhaps most important, she realized, was that when she was with him she didn't think about Season all the time. She began to see a possibility of life beyond Season, a life in which she didn't startle every time she saw a blond head on a slender female body. She would never forget the horror of that summer and fall, but someday it might just be a distant memory—something that had happened, instead of something that might happen again. She pressed herself up against Adam's arm.

That would be something worth fighting for.

Rebecca wasn't a very strict observer of the Jewish faith, but Kerry had bought her a Hanukkah present anyway: a digital camera. Kerry figured it was something that would take Rebecca outside herself, would force her to interact with the rest of the world, even if from behind a barrier of metal and glass. Of course, she didn't detail her reasoning for Rebecca, who loved the gift.

They had taken it to the boardwalk on a bright, sunny early morning at the end of the semester, the day before Rebecca was to leave for New York to be with her family. Rebecca was framing a shot of the roller coaster when her cell phone broke into song. She handed the camera to Kerry and tugged the phone from her coat pocket. "Hello?"

Kerry watched Rebecca's face change. Her mood had been good today, cheerful, and she'd answered the phone with a smile. But as she listened to the voice on the other end, her smile crumpled into something else. Her lower lip started to quiver, her eyes widened, her forehead creased like a freshly plowed field. After listening for a minute, she handed the phone to Kerry and walked away.

"Hello?" Kerry asked, inadvertently echoing Rebecca's response.

"Hey, Kerry." It was Scott Banner's voice, but he sounded anxious, upset.

"What's wrong, Scott?"

"I—I found her, Kerry. I found Season. She's in New Hampshire. But—well, can you come out here? Fast? She hasn't seen me yet, but I'm afraid she will."

"Sure, of course," Kerry said. "Soon as I can get a flight. Be sure you stay safe, okay?"

"I'm trying," Scott promised. "But I don't want to lose her either."

"I know, but staying out of her way is the most important thing. How did you find her?"

"A wild guess," Scott said. "I figured, you know, winter, ski resorts. I've been making the rounds up here and finally spotted her."

"That's amazing," Kerry said. The familiar and terrifying notion that maybe Season wanted to be found came to her—the idea that Season wanted to pick them off, one by one. "But listen, you keep a low profile. She's dangerous." *To say the least.*

"I know, Kerry."

Yeah, he knows, she thought. *But he went there anyway, by himself, looking for her. What was he thinking?*

It wouldn't help to harangue him. She just needed to keep him safe somehow. "Have you told Brandy?"

"I was going to call her next," he said. "I figure we need all hands on deck."

"No," Kerry said sharply. "If you haven't told her, don't." She looked at Rebecca, who stood fifty yards away on the beach, her red coat and yellow cargos standing out in sharp contrast to the blue-gray sea and blue sky. A stiff wind whipped her hair, and she looked very small against the wide background. "I'm not going to bring Rebecca, either. I don't want to put them in any danger if I don't have to."

"But . . . Kerry . . . ," he began.

"I know what I'm doing, Scott." *Which is a lie, of course, but maybe he'll buy it.* "You're just going to have to trust me."

"Okay," he said. "The nearest airport is a tiny one in Laconia, so get a flight into there and then call me. I'll keep tabs on her until then."

"I'll let you know when to expect me. Good job tracking her down."

"Thanks, Kerr." He sounded a little more relaxed than when she had first taken the phone.

"And you be careful!"

"You don't have to worry about that," he assured her.

I already am, she thought.

Kerry said good-bye and ended the call. Rebecca was still down on the beach, looking out at the sea with her arms wrapped around herself. Kerry walked down toward her, but the thunder of the surf and rush of the wind covered the sound of her approach. When she touched Rebecca's shoulder, the girl almost screamed.

"Jeez, Kerry, you scared the crap out of me!" When she turned around, Kerry saw that she had been crying. Mascara streaked her face.

"I'm sorry," Kerry said, spreading her arms. Rebecca moved into them and they shared a hug. Kerry's long black hair flew around them, mixing with Rebecca's, shorter and red. Kerry couldn't help remembering her first kiss with Daniel, also on a beach, several hundred miles to the south. "I didn't mean to startle you, Beck."

"It's okay," Rebecca said into Kerry's shoulder. She pulled away and looked into Kerry's eyes, her own brown ones still moist. "So, should I pack for New Hampshire?"

"No."

Rebecca's face brightened immediately, like the sun breaking through clouds. "You mean it? We're not going after her this time?"

"You're not," Kerry explained. "You've got to go to New York. I'm going alone."

The clouds returned. "Kerry, no!"

"I have to, Rebecca. Scott can't handle her

by himself, and the longer he stays there the more danger he's in."

"Then why doesn't he just clear out of there?" Rebecca insisted, tears beginning to flow again. "Who says she has to be our problem?"

Kerry dug her sneaker in the sand. "She's our problem because we inherited her. She's our problem because she killed Mace and Daniel and Josh. And because it looks like maybe she's tracking us down, one at a time. Which means that Scott could be in a lot of trouble if I don't get there soon."

Rebecca's mouth hardened. "And what can you do about her, Kerry? You said you and Mother Blessing together couldn't take her."

"Yeah, well, that's just something I'll have to figure out when I get there," Kerry said.

"There's no way I can talk you out of this?"

"No, Rebecca. I don't really know how to explain—it's like, my destiny is linked with Season's now. As long as she's out there, my life isn't completely my own. I have to go."

Rebecca sniffled and wiped her eyes with her hand. "Doesn't mean I'm not going to try," she vowed.

"All the way to the airport if you want," Kerry agreed.

They stopped by Rebecca's house on the way out. Kerry said good-bye to Erin, Rebecca's housemate, whom she had only seen a handful of times since arriving, and packed up her few belongings. Once again she would get on an airplane that would take her toward Season Howe. She knew Rebecca's arguments made sense—if she just told Scott to get out of there, if they never went after Season again, she might just forget about them, right? Let them live out their lives in peace?

Maybe. And then again, maybe she really was hunting them. Maybe it wasn't happenstance that Scott found her, and Josh before that. If that was the case, then leaving her alone didn't help any of them.

Besides, Kerry wanted answers almost as much as she wanted revenge. She had been killing time in Santa Cruz, cooling her heels and getting stale, without even realizing it. Now she had a direction again, a purpose.

Scott had spent days cruising ski resorts before he spotted her. Countless blondes, many with stocking caps covering their hair, had passed before his eyes. He was growing frustrated, starting to think the whole plan was just crazy. *There's an entire world to choose from,* he thought. *Why would she pick New England just because it's convenient for me?*

At the same time, the longer his hunt stretched out, the more relaxed he became. He forgot, for brief periods of time, about the gun in his jacket pocket, though the memory of it always crashed back over him like a tidal wave of anxiety. He enjoyed the fit, attractive bodies around him, in more colors of spandex and nylon than he had known existed. The sun, the clean mountain air, the pure white snow, and the physical beauty, both of the natural region and the resort buildings themselves, all lulled him into a kind of contented languor. He was sipping a Coke in a huge, soft chair near a roaring fire in a lodge, its walls log and stone, when he saw an attractive blonde walking past the window with a pair of skis balanced on her shoulder, clad in a snug black ski outfit.

For a quarter of a second Scott forgot why he was even here. He appreciated her beauty and had a moment's sense of familiarity.

Abruptly, though, he realized *why* she was familiar, and more urgently, why it mattered. He slammed the Coke down on the closest table, left a few bucks for the waitress, and wove around skiers until he found a door.

Outside, of course, the air was frigid and the walkway jammed with people, many, like the blonde he'd seen, carrying their skis. Scott looked around frantically. He had only caught a glimpse of her, and it had been months since that day in San Diego. He could easily have been wrong.

But at the moment that he had thought that the woman was Season, his whole body went cold. It was, in the words of the old cliché, as if someone had walked over his grave. Which always seemed a little strange, since why would that be a problem to someone who wasn't dead yet?

Still, it seemed suddenly, disturbingly appropriate. Scott put his hand inside his jacket pocket, closed it on the little nine-mil he carried there. Its cold steel brought him scant comfort.

He dodged and ducked, and finally he spotted the familiar form. Her clothes were skintight spandex, but she had taken off her cap and tucked it into a pocket. She stood at a coffee cart with her back to him. Scott slowed his pace and walked past the cart, then, trying to appear far more casual than he felt, he stopped and turned, looking past the cart at the blonde.

There could be no mistaking that face—the cheekbones, the vivid, almost cobalt blue eyes, like infinite sky, framed by short golden hair that curled toward a strong jaw.

It was the face of Season Howe.

He spun away quickly, before she could spot him. She was a dozen feet away. The gun was suddenly hot in his hand. He could walk up to her before she left the cart, or with her hands full of hot coffee and skis. A couple of shots in the head, close range. Sure, he'd go to prison, and it would kind of mess up the whole plan of ending up with Kerry.

But he would also be putting an end to a monster. Preventing a killer from killing again. There was something to be said for that.

Even if Kerry had to visit him in jail.

The gun was loaded, the safety off—he double-checked that with his thumb, inside his pocket. He'd never actually fired the thing, but he had practiced inside his Plymouth motel room for the last few nights. He understood it in theory, if not in practice.

Besides, how hard can it be?

In spite of the cold air, Scott felt sweat pouring from him. His hand slipped on the gun's grip. The world seemed like it was spinning too fast, colors whirling around him. He was light-headed and nothing sounded right, his ears rang as if he was deep underwater. He took a few steps toward Season but his knees felt like jelly, his feet wouldn't connect firmly with the ground.

It wasn't going to work. Before he reached Season—before, he hoped, Season saw him—Scott turned away, walked in the other direction until he found a vacant seat on a bench. *Who am I trying to kid?* he wondered. *I'm no gunman.* With shaking hands he drew his cell phone from its inside pocket, glad he had Rebecca's number programmed in. No way he'd be able to dial right now.

He punched send and waited.

Kerry would know what to do.

7

Kerry Profitt's diary, December 23.

I'm almost getting used to writing in this journal on
airplanes going to or from an encounter with Season
Howe. I say almost because it's always an adventure
seeing how far the person sitting in front of me is
going to push his seat back, and whether I can actually see the screen as I type. This particular one is
really pushing his luck—just about asking for someone to flick the bald spot on his head with her finger.
I guess that someone would be me. Lucky for him I'm
not the violent sort.

Or am I? It occurs to me (a little late, maybe?
Am I not examining my life enough or something?)
that I have spent most of the last five months, going
on half a year, on an effort—unsuccessful so far—to
commit a violent act against a person. A person I

have plenty of reason to be mad at, but whom I really don't know.

That's not like me—at least, not like the me I used to be. I don't know if "meek" would be the word I'd have used to describe me. "Mild"? Maybe. I have always had a stubborn streak, and if something got in the way of getting what I thought was important, I was willing to do whatever it took, steamroller anyone. (Poor Ms. Tomkins, back in 8th grade, who really didn't understand how important my friends and I thought it was to have an anime club in school. A short-lived fad, at least where I was concerned. But man, did we hound her.) But actual violence? One of the reasons I lost interest in anime was the amount of violence in it.

So I guess there's a new me in town. I'll try to decide if I like her or not.

Glancing at the business type sitting in the seat next to me, also laptopping. Only on his there are, like, spreadsheets and numbers and stuff that looks suspiciously like work. I haven't done any of that since the Seaside Resort, and I can hardly remember what it feels like to cash a paycheck.

That's okay—I bet Mr. Business Type doesn't know what it feels like to cast a spell. He probably doesn't even believe in magic, which is so ingrained in me now I can hardly remember NOT believing in magic. Seems so . . . naïve, now. People don't believe because they don't want to believe. Because the world is simpler, they think, without it.

Well, tell you what, people. The world is a freaking complicated place. Magic doesn't make that more or less true. But with magic, if I need to, I can make you think I've had a shower and changed my clothes in the last twenty-four, even if I haven't. Let's see you top that with technology.

Ha!

More later.

K.

It turned out to be not so easy to fly from San Jose to Laconia, as Scott had recommended. Instead Kerry flew into Chicago's O'Hare, from which she phoned Aunt Betty to tell her she was fine. From Chicago she flew into Manchester, New Hampshire, and then hung around for several hours until she could catch a puddle jumper into Laconia.

There were only ten seats on the plane, of which four were occupied. The single flight attendant made Kerry and her three fellow passengers spread out on the little plane to make sure it was balanced, an idea that filled Kerry with dread, and then it took off, lurching and bouncing all the way into Laconia. The town turned out to be relatively flat, though surrounded by lakes, including Lake Winnipesaukee, which was large but maybe, Kerry thought, not quite as big as its name.

It was almost midnight when she arrived, and she was both exhausted and anxious. The closer they came to landing in Laconia, the more frightened she became. She remembered Las Vegas, when everyone but Josh had hung around the airport waiting for her. She would probably never know just how late they had been, but she guessed it was only minutes—minutes that had cost Josh Quinn his life.

Now, with Scott's life potentially in the balance, Kerry couldn't dial his phone number fast enough. He answered on the second ring.

"Kerry?"

"Hi, Scott. I'm here. Where are you?"

"You're in Laconia?"

"Right. At the airport here."

"Okay, you're going to have to get a car," he said. "You're still almost an hour away."

An hour? Anything can happen in an hour, Kerry thought. "Are you safe?" she asked. "Do you know where she is?"

"I think so," Scott said. "She's in a hotel room here at Loon Mountain. I couldn't get a room in the same place, but I've been hanging around as much as I can. Haven't been kicked out yet."

"And she doesn't know you're there?"

"I'm pretty sure not. She seems to be enjoying herself and not paying any attention to me."

Kerry felt a flash of anger at that idea. *Enjoying herself. While we run around like mad, just trying to stay sane and alive, she's up in the mountains having fun.*

"Okay," she said. "Tell me how to get there."

She wasn't sure how she would get a car— no one was likely to rent to her, even if there had been any rental places open at this hour. She looked frantically around the terminal building, and finally a dour-looking man—central casting New England, she thought—ambled toward her with a broom in his hands. He wore a janitor's uniform with a name patch that said MITCH. "You look like you're lost, miss," he said. "Somethin' I can do?"

"I'm trying to get to a place called Loon Mountain," she said.

He spoke slowly, and there was something on his face that might have been a smile. *Or maybe gas,* she thought. "Well, you could wait till mornin'. Be a bus then."

"That's great," she replied sarcastically. "But I really have to get there tonight. As fast as possible."

Moving just as slowly as he spoke, Mitch glanced at a clock. "Well, I get off at twelve," he said. "I could give you a ride up there, you want."

"It's after twelve," Kerry pointed out. The clock read 12:06.

"Ayup, that it is. Just workin' late," Mitch said. "I don't sleep too good these nights."

He apparently doesn't tell time too good, either, Kerry noted, but she didn't want to mention that if he was going to do her a favor. She recognized the danger inherent in accepting a ride from a stranger, on a dark night, into unfamiliar mountains. But then, the hitchhiking thing had gone okay. And she figured she could handle Mitch if he got out of hand. If he drove like he did everything else, she could probably get out and run at any point and still make better time than he could.

"Okay, I guess," she said. "Are you going that way?"

"Nobody's goin' that way. That's your whole problem, isn't it?"

"Well, yes, I suppose it is."

He carried the broom over to a janitor's closet. "Wait right there, miss," he said. "I'll be back directly."

Kerry spent the few moments that he was gone running through self-defense spells in her head. She felt comfortable with them. Unless old Mitch turned out to be a witch, there was nothing he could do to hurt her. And if he tried anything, then she'd wind up driving after all, and he'd have a long walk home.

A minute later he came back from the closet wearing an anorak and tugging on furry gloves. He made that expression again, like someone trying on a new smile to see if it fit. "You ready to go?"

"I've been ready," she said.

"Kind of impatient, aren't you?" he asked.

"You could say that."

"I just did."

Kerry tried to walk fast, but Mitch just kind of shuffled along at his own pace, and she knew she couldn't get too far ahead since she didn't know where they were going. Once they were in the parking lot, it became clear—there were only a scattered handful of vehicles there, and Mitch plodded toward the oldest one, a truck that might have been state-of-the-art in the 1950s, but not since. He opened the passenger door for Kerry and then climbed in behind the wheel.

"You say you're in a hurry?" he asked her, although he knew full well, she was sure, what the answer would be.

"You know, that old life and death thing," she answered.

He put the ancient truck into gear and stomped on the accelerator. The truck left rubber behind in the parking lot and roared onto the street. "Well, then I reckon we ought to get a move on," he said. He kept both hands on the wheel in a death grip, as if afraid it would get away from him if he relaxed. But dark, sleepy Laconia zipped past outside the windows much faster than Kerry would have believed possible. Within fifteen minutes they were climbing up into the White Mountains. Snow gleamed silver, reflecting the moon overhead, trees strobed past, and Mitch drove silently, his eyes forward, his lips pressed together. Kerry figured that his picture would be in the dictionary under "taciturn," maybe cross-referenced with "crusty."

But she wasn't going to complain. The guy was going more than an hour out of his way just to get her where she needed to go. He hadn't mentioned money, or any other reward, and he hadn't asked her any questions. She was grateful for his help and delighted that a human being would make the effort to assist another in this cynical age.

About forty minutes after they had left the airport, Mitch pointed out the windshield at an array of buildings glowing in the darkness. "Loon Mountain Lodge," he said.

"Wow, that was fast."

"What you wanted, right?"

"That's right," Kerry agreed. She dug her

phone out. "I've got to find out where my friend is."

"Asleep, if he knows what's good for him," Mitch commented.

"Well, if he knew that he wouldn't be here at all," Kerry said. "That's never been his strong point."

"People don't know how important sleep is," Mitch said. "Take it from me."

"I've had plenty the last couple of weeks," Kerry told him. "But I don't always. I know what you mean." She dialed Scott and he picked up immediately.

"Where are you?" he asked.

"We're here, basically," she said. "Where are you?"

"Come to the parking lot closest to the lodge," Scott replied. "I'm in the RAV4. Look in the second row."

Kerry relayed the directions to Mitch. "Okay, we're just about there." She disconnected and scanned the snow-laden cars, trucks, and SUVs. Near the end of the row, she saw his black Toyota. "There it is!" she shouted. As they pulled up, Scott got out of the vehicle. He wore a dark blue down coat with the hood pulled up, a knit cap on his head beneath the hood, jeans, and snow boots. His breath steamed as he stood by the SUV, waiting.

"That's him?" Mitch asked. "Looks cold."

"That's him," Kerry agreed happily. "Thank you so much for the ride. Can I pay for gas or something?"

"Nope," Mitch answered. "I'd stayed at the airport I'd've been makin' messes just to have somethin' to clean up. You just have sense enough to get in out of the cold, that's all I ask."

"It's a deal." She shook Mitch's big hand—slowly—and then climbed down from the truck. As soon as her feet hit icy pavement, Scott enveloped her in a hug.

"Kerry," he breathed. "I'm so glad you're here."

Kerry couldn't help laughing. "You must be freezing," she declared. "Haven't you been running the heat?"

"Off and on," Scott admitted. "But I haven't wanted to sit there with the engine running because I figured that would attract attention."

"Can we go inside?" Kerry asked. She was

an Illinois girl, used to harsh plains winters, but time in California and southern Virginia seemed to have thinned her blood. She rubbed her arms vigorously through her heavy coat. "It is really cold out here."

"We could," Scott said. "But there are various doors out of the building. Unless Season's planning to leave on skis, she'll have to take the road. We can see it from here, but if we're inside we could miss her."

"Maybe. But if we turn into a couple of corpsesicles out here, she could waltz right past us anyway."

Scott nodded. "Good point."

"Do you have any reason to think she's going to skip out tonight?" Kerry wondered.

He contemplated a moment before answering. "She put in a pretty full day on the slopes," he said. "Ate a big dinner, couple glasses of wine."

"Sounds like you kept a close eye on her," Kerry commented.

"I did what I could without being too obvious. Anyway, I figure once she hits the sack, she's there to stay. At least, that's what a human would do."

"She's a witch, but she's still human. Just . . . differently abled, as they say."

"Well, whatever she is, I bet she's sound asleep. Like we should be."

"Will we be too obvious if we go in now?"

"It's, what, a little after one? The bars are still open in there. We'll fit in."

He locked up the RAV4 and they started the trudge up to the lodge. "By the way," he said as they walked. "Merry Christmas Eve."

"Oh, yeah." She had forgotten, in her weariness and worry, that when midnight hit it had become Christmas Eve. "Heck of a way to spend a holiday, huh?"

Scott put a gloved hand on her shoulder. "I'm not complaining."

8

The Loon Mountain Lodge was all peaked roofs and large windows. Some faced onto the parking lot, but the best looked out toward the slopes. When they got inside Kerry saw that Scott had been correct—in spite of the late hour, there were still plenty of merry-makers inside wishing one another happy holidays. It wouldn't last; they wouldn't be able to stay inside all night, she knew, without getting a room. And Scott had said the hotel was full. So they'd be heading back to the RAV4 in a while. But at least until then they could warm their bones a little.

Neither one was old enough to get into the bar, but there was enough spillover into the lobby that they felt comfortable just taking a seat there. A fire crackled in a big stone fireplace with a wooden mantel, scenting the air with the tang of wood smoke. On the mantel, pine branches decorated with glass Christmas balls crowded a couple of antique duck decoys. In a corner away from the fire stood a Christmas tree, at least ten feet tall, fully decorated, with giant boxes strewn underneath it as if waiting for the next morning.

Scott sat close to Kerry, his knees touching hers. His cheeks were flushed with the cold, his eyes glittering. Something about him seemed different than when she had last seen him, in Las Vegas after Josh's death. He seemed more . . . alive, maybe. Like his internal batteries had been running low, but were now recharged.

Kerry had only had a few short conversations with him since then, too involved in her own life, she guessed, to delve into his. She felt uncomfortable bringing up Brandy, but didn't see any way around it. "I'm sorry," she began. "About, you know, Brandy."

Scott nodded, then shrugged. "Life happens," he said. "She was ready to try something different, I guess. I'm doing okay, though. I think maybe I was ready for it too, but just didn't know it yet."

"Are you . . . seeing anyone?" she asked.

"No." His answer was immediate and emphatic. "No, not at all. She is, I guess. I don't know him, but she's mentioned a guy named Adam a couple of times."

"Are you okay with that?"

"Like I have a choice? Sure, I'm okay. Just time to move on, right? I guess you haven't had time for any . . ." He let the question trail off, but she knew what he meant.

The truth was, since Daniel had died she had hardly thought about romance at all. He was the man she had wanted to be with, the only one she had ever met with whom she could imagine a future. "Nope. No time at all."

"You'll . . . you'll find the right guy," Scott assured her. "You'll probably find out he was right there the whole time, and you just didn't know it. You've just had a lot on your plate."

"That's for sure," she agreed.

"Listen, I should tell you," he said, changing the subject abruptly. "When I came here, I brought a gun. I was going to kill her."

"Season?" She couldn't keep the surprise from her voice.

"Of course, Season. What, you don't think a gun could kill her?"

"I know it can't," Kerry stated firmly. "Mother Blessing shot her four times with a rifle, close up. She just spat the bullets out into her hand."

It was Scott's turn to be surprised. His color had already started to pale from being inside, out of the cold, but now he blanched. "You're kidding me."

"Not at all." She sat back in the seat—he moved to stay close to her, she noticed—and told him the whole story of the battle outside Mother Blessing's cabin in the swamp.

When she was finished, his hand was on her knee, squeezing it. "I don't see how you could have done all that, Kerry," he said. "I'd have been absolutely terrified."

"What makes you think I wasn't?"

Late-night had turned to middle-of-the night while they talked, and the bar crowd had started to thin. "We should get out of here," Kerry observed. "They're going to charge us for a room pretty soon. Can we stay warm enough in your car?"

"I've got a blanket," he answered. "I think if we huddle we'll be all right."

"Okay then. Huddle it is." She rose and led

him out of the building. It bothered her that Season was inside sleeping—she wanted to go back in and bring things to a head right now, but she knew that wasn't the way to go. Instead, they went to Scott's RAV4, put the seats back as far as they'd go, and snuggled close to one another underneath his blanket. He ran the heater for a few minutes until the car warmed up a bit, and soon they were toasty.

Scott had never been Kerry's idea of gorgeous. But it had been a long time since she'd had a man's body pressed against her. Feeling his warmth and solid bulk, she found the idea of kissing him swimming to the forefront of her thoughts. By the time it occurred to her, though, his breathing was regular and deep. He was out. Kerry tried to stay awake, to keep watch, but the day had been long and she was worn out. Within minutes, they were both sound asleep.

Kerry assumed that the skiers getting the earliest starts were not the ones who had been up drinking all night, but there were plenty of them. She woke up feeling pretty well rested despite the difficult conditions and late night, but famished and needing some grooming time. She was dying to take a shower and wash her hair, which had been tied back into a ponytail since she'd left California the day before. *Shampoo would be great,* she thought. *And conditioner. And an exfoliating scrub . . .*

Thinking like that wouldn't help. She shook Scott awake.

"Hey," she said brightly. "It's Christmas Eve. I'm starving, and if I don't brush my teeth my breath is going to kill somebody. Let's go inside."

Scott blinked a few times and found his glasses on the dash. "Okay," he said. "I could go for food. And dental hygiene."

They went back inside and found a restaurant where they could eat and watch the lobby, just in case Season woke early too. They still hadn't seen her when they were done. Over the last of their coffee, Kerry brought up what she knew would be a difficult subject.

"It's time for you to head out, Scott."

"What do you mean, head out?"

"I mean . . . when I confront Season this time, it's got to be alone. I need to do this by myself."

He looked at her like he couldn't believe what he had heard. "By yourself? You can't!"

"I have to. There's no other way for it to work." She didn't describe exactly what her plan was, but he'd never go along with it anyway. That was why she needed him gone.

"Kerry, no."

"Scott. It's not a request. I'm sorry, but you've got to go."

He was still shaking his head, still not going along with it. She was going to have to be harsh, she feared. It was for his own good. There was no telling what fireworks might happen when she confronted Season.

"I can—whatever you need me to do, Kerry, I'll do it," he insisted. "Just let me stay with you."

"You can't, Scott. It won't work. I'm glad you found her, that was great. And I appreciate you keeping me warm all night and everything. But your part is done now, and it's my turn."

"Your turn? Kerry, it's always you. Why not let me help?"

"You've done the part you can do." Kerry was firm. "Now the best thing you can do to help is to go away, before she comes out."

Scott frowned angrily. "Okay," he said, getting up in a huff. "If that's how you want it, that's what you get. I thought we were partners here, but I guess not."

"That's right," Kerry said. "No partners this time out. It's a solo deal."

"Whatever," he said. He grabbed his backpack off the restaurant floor. "I hope you're not making a big mistake," he said as he stormed away.

Oh, you and me both, Kerry thought. She hated to make him angry, but he'd never have left otherwise. And as much as it hurt her to see him so upset, he really was better off.

Now, of course, came the really hard part. It had been one thing to make a big show of courage and resolve in order to drive Scott away. But she had to follow through—she had to confront Season, all by herself, and not let the resolve she had faked so convincingly turn into outright terror.

Hands trembling, she left the restaurant and went back into the lobby to wait for Season.

Fortunately the wait wasn't too long—otherwise, Kerry believed, she might have lost her nerve altogether. But less than twenty minutes after paying the breakfast bill and finding a chair in the lobby, she saw Season's sleek form, clad in tight royal blue ski attire, heading for the back door.

Swallowing hard, steeling herself for anything, Kerry followed Season outside. She wanted to catch the witch before she got too far, and definitely before she realized Kerry was here. Catching her off-guard seemed like the only way this had even a chance of working.

"Season!" she said sharply once they were both outside. She thought Season tensed for a moment—a sudden lifting of shoulder blades, straightening of spine—but then she kept walking. *Not going by that name here, then,* Kerry reasoned. *But she'll answer to it anyway.* She moved closer to Season, who had increased her pace.

"Season Howe," she said again. This time her voice was lower. She knew Season would be listening for it.

And this time Season turned—casually, as if just looking around to admire the beautiful morning—and faced her. Her expression didn't reveal any surprise or consternation—she had a pleasant smile fixed on her pretty face, and it stayed there while she regarded Kerry. Still casual, she moved some of her neatly trimmed honey-blond hair off her face. "I'm surprised to see you," she said. Her voice was soft, almost friendly.

She's good, Kerry thought. *Anyone watching us would think we were old pals.*

"I want to talk," Kerry assured her. "That's all, just talk."

"I don't think we really have anything to say to each other."

"Oh, you're wrong, Season. We have plenty of things to discuss, trust me."

Season laughed. "Have you ever given me a reason to trust you?"

"I've never given you any reason not to."

"You've tried to kill me."

Kerry's turn to laugh. "Point taken. And vice versa, I have to say."

"Maybe I should do it again now," Season said. "I could, you know."

"I know that," Kerry said. "I know you could try, at least. But I know a few tricks now too." Which was almost a lie—she knew nothing now that she hadn't that last day in the swamp. She hadn't quite exhausted her repertoire that time, because Mother Blessing had been calling the shots. But she hadn't picked up anything new since then.

Season smiled again. "Enough to stop me? Show me."

They were talking on a busy walkway, with skiers bustling past them on their way to the lifts. So far no one had paid them any attention, because their poses and attitudes were nonchalant. Kerry wanted to keep it that way, but it was looking like Season would need some convincing if she were not to blast Kerry on the spot.

She needed to demonstrate her skills, but in a way that would not draw any notice. Beside her was a wooden railing, with a snowy expanse beyond that led to the base of the slopes. Not far away, cable lifts ferried skiers up to the runs, which were already strewn with colorful specks, like sprinkles on a frosted doughnut, except that these sprinkles were moving swiftly downhill. Close to the lodge, the snow was dotted with trees and rocks. She ticked her head toward it, and Season's gaze followed. Kerry concentrated, gesturing toward the ground, and said, "*Ashashalika*," one of the old words of magic.

Rocks shifted, shaking off their dusting of snow. Big ones rolled quickly to the points Kerry had visualized, and smaller ones filled in the spaces between. When they had settled, they spelled out SH in the snow.

Season laughed again, a sound that Kerry realized was a pleasant one. Season was pretty, she was cultured, she had good manners. It was just too bad she was an evil killer.

"Cute," she said. "But how does it keep me from killing you?"

"It doesn't," Kerry admitted. "But I can't show you that kind of thing without drawing a lot of eyeballs this way. I don't think either of us wants that."

"You're probably right," Season said. "But I could cloak us, and kill you just the same."

"Oh, cloaking," Kerry said, feigning surprise. She had pulled it off, drawn Season right where she wanted her. "If you want cloaking, look." She brought her hands together, touched her thumbs, and then spread them wide, which dissipated one of the cloaking spells that had kept her real stunt from Season's eyes. As far as any other onlookers were concerned, she and Season were just standing and talking—Mother Blessing had taught her that the real test of a witch's cloaking skills was the ability to reveal something to one person or group while keeping it hidden from others.

But what Season saw was a cartoon-style weight labeled 16 TONS hanging in the air, inches above her head.

"Oh, bravo," Season said, clapping her hands. "Misdirection *and* a genuine threat, cloaked. You're better than I thought."

Coming from Season Howe, that was real praise, and Kerry felt a flush of pride. "Thanks," she said. Another word of the old tongue, another gesture, and the weight had vanished, the rocks returned to their original positions.

Season regarded her closely for a moment, her head shaking slowly from side to side. "You really have a lot of guts to do this," she said. "Or you're stupider than you look. And I don't think that's the case."

"No, it would be a bad idea to count on that."

"We should get out of here, then," Season suggested. "If we're going to talk, I mean."

"I kind of like it public," Kerry countered, still trying to sound bolder than she felt. "How do I know you wouldn't take me someplace just to kill me?"

"I guess you don't," Season replied, turning the tables. "You'll just have to trust me."

9

Scott couldn't believe what Kerry had said to him. Everything he had done was for her. Hunting Season, finding her, keeping her in sight all day—even risking his life by buying that stupid gun. All for Kerry . . . and then she just dumped him from the whole thing. *Get lost, basically. Go away, little boy, you've done your chore for the day. Merry Christmas Eve, but I'm done with you.*

As if that wasn't bad enough, she had completely ignored the subtext of his remarks, blown it off as if she hadn't understood. He was offering himself to her, and she either didn't notice or wasn't interested. She had a lot on her mind, so it was possible, even probable that she might have missed some cues. And it probably came out of left field—

he didn't know if she had ever been aware of his attraction to her.

Still, he didn't think he'd been overly subtle. Especially with the whole snuggling through the night thing. He thought it was one of the best nights of his life—fraught with the terror of possible discovery by Season, and on the cold side, but still . . . amazing just to be near to Kerry.

And then she just turned it all away. Sent him packing.

Well, she might not think he had anything to contribute, but he knew better.

He walked all the way out to the RAV4, furious at her. He tossed his backpack into the cargo area and was about to get in behind the driver's seat when he thought better of it. *Who says she gets to make the rules?* Scott wondered. He stuffed his keys back into his pocket and returned to the hotel. Much as he had done with Season, he stayed out of Kerry's view but kept an eye on her. It was only a few minutes until Season showed up and Kerry chased her outside.

He hadn't been able to get close enough to hear, but he could see just fine. They feigned a perfectly friendly conversation, but from Kerry's body language and some of her movements, he knew there was more to it than met the eye. Then Season led Kerry away—straight toward the parking lot. Scott had to spin away and insert himself between a couple of skiers to make sure they didn't spot him, but after their backs were turned he followed.

Outside, Season led Kerry to a black Jeep 4X4. Scott ran to the RAV4, jumped in, and cranked the engine. By the time Season was leaving the parking lot, he was three cars behind. He opened his cell phone and dialed.

"Hello?" she answered a moment later. "Scott?"

"Brandy, listen, I know you don't want me calling you, but this is important. Season Howe just kidnapped Kerry."

"Kidnapped? What are you talking about, Scott? Where are you?"

"I'm at Loon Mountain, in New Hampshire," he said, the words spilling out of him in a torrent. "I came up here looking for Season, and I found her. So I called Kerry. She came out, and then she wanted to confront Season by herself. But I watched. I think they did some magic stuff, and then Season took her away in a Jeep. I'm following them."

"Scott," Brandy said, and her concern sounded genuine. "You be really careful. I know you like Kerry, but she's different than we are now. She has powers that we don't. She can take care of herself."

"She can't take Season by herself."

"You don't know that."

"Yes, I do," Scott protested. He had to make a hard left turn, so he held the phone between his cheek and shoulder while he did. "She told me this story—she and Mother Blessing together couldn't beat Season, and that was only a few weeks ago. Before she went to stay with Rebecca."

Brandy was quiet for a second, taking that in. "Okay. So where are you, exactly?"

"I'm driving. I'm following them. North on I-93."

"But they don't know you're behind them?"

"I sure hope not."

"Make sure you keep it that way. If Kerry sees you back there, Season will figure it out."

Scott eyed the horizon ahead. Storm

clouds glowered; the sky was a ferocious leaden gray. "It looks like the weather is turning, too," he reported.

"Scott, I'm coming up there. It'll take me a while from here, but I'll leave as soon as I can."

"If you're going to come up, Brandy," Scott replied, "maybe you should call Rebecca. Kerry said she's in New York visiting her folks. Maybe she can come too. The more the better."

"Okay, I'll try her," Brandy promised. "And I'll have my phone, so keep me posted. And be careful!"

He ended the call. People kept telling him to be careful, like he was some kind of simpleton. Kerry had warned him to be careful, and look where it got her. Snatched by Season and driven up into the mountains.

It occurred to him to try Kerry's phone. He punched her number, and it rang three times before she answered it.

"Kerry, is everything okay?" he asked.

"Yes, Scott. Everything is fine."

"Can you talk freely?"

"Sure, why not?" She sounded normal, relaxed. Not like Season was holding a mystical gun to her head.

"I was just wondering. If you need me for anything, you can call me. You know that, right?"

"I know, Scott. Thanks."

"Okay. Talk to you later." He ended the call, feeling like an idiot. Either she was being kidnapped or she wasn't. Would a kidnapper let her keep her cell phone? Maybe, if she knew it couldn't help her.

He hung back, at least a half mile behind— just far enough to keep them in sight from time to time, but not so close that they'd realize they were being followed. The radio brought in a mixture of reggae, ska, and punk from a college station in Manchester, keeping him alert. After an hour or so, the station began to fade, and snowflakes started to slap against his windshield. They didn't stick, but before long he had to turn on his headlights and wipers. He started to feel hungry. He could use a bathroom. And his shoulders were getting sore from the driving. But they kept going, so he did. Season had left the interstate but continued on what seemed to be a fairly major two-lane highway.

His mind whirled with conflicting

thoughts of Kerry. He was sick with worry about her. Had Season hypnotized her, or enchanted her somehow? Why else would she get in a car with a known killer—one she had battled just weeks before?

And then those thoughts mixed with his memories of earlier—of the joy he had felt when he'd seen her step down from that old truck. Even in the dim light of the parking lot, her big green eyes had seemed to glow, her smile radiating like a small sun. His heart had swelled at the sight of her and at the sensation of holding her in his arms—and of her returning the hug—when they'd embraced. Her scent filled him with a happiness he could barely believe.

He wasn't sure if other people felt things with the intensity he did, but he had often suspected not. For others, emotion sometimes seemed secondary to the regular grind of life. Brandy, for instance, prioritized feelings after intellect, after psychology, or her interpretation of it. And his own parents loved each other, or said they did, and had been married for more than a quarter of a century. But while they tried to have dinner together a couple of nights a week, one or the other always seemed to be off at a meeting or function that the other wasn't part of. Work or obligations got the best of people, he believed, forcing them to put off their emotional lives and well-being for later, which couldn't be healthy.

But not Scott. He found himself trying sometimes—making an effort to, as Brandy said, sublimate his feelings. But they wouldn't be put in a box. They *were* him—surface, inside, everything. The rest of him was just the clothes they were dressed in.

And right now his emotions were a stew of love and terror—but they were rapidly being mixed with anxiety about driving in the worsening storm.

When Season and Kerry pulled off the highway he almost missed them. He had spaced out, the snow creating a field of pure white ahead of him, and his focus was all on not losing the road. So when he realized that he couldn't see their taillights anymore, it was almost too late. At the last moment he spotted the small side road leading off to the right, higher up into the White Mountains. He yanked the wheel hard, and the SUV's rear wheels started to fishtail out from under him. He corrected by turning into the skid, and brought the vehicle under control in time to avoid going off the road or flipping over. If anyone had been coming up fast behind him, it would have been trouble. And there was precious little traffic—if he'd gone off the road, it could have been a long time before someone found him. He let go of the wheel long enough to wipe the sweat from his eyes, then nosed the RAV4 toward the side road.

The wind was really blowing now, coating everything with snow. Tracks showed on this little road, but there was already snow sticking to the blacktop, beginning to cover them up. Trees and bushes and hillsides were frosted as thickly as a wedding cake.

At least there was just one way they could have gone. The road only led up.

Scott pressed down on the accelerator. His wheels slid on the snow and ice, but then they caught and carried him forward. He realized, too late, that he hadn't even noticed if this road had a name, or a sign—if he had to tell Brandy how to find him up here, he'd be out of luck.

Wipers flailing, he drove on through a

nearly impenetrable curtain of snow. He was getting genuinely worried now—this was starting to look like a blizzard, or a whiteout. If he was stranded up here, without food or water or shelter, he could be in some serious trouble.

But Kerry already was, he was convinced. He couldn't back off.

The road wound up a mountain, becoming narrower. Trees hemmed it in on both sides, looming dark and menacing in the dim light. The roadway was completely covered by snow now, and his tracks seemed to fill as soon as he passed.

So when he reached a fork in the road, he had no idea which way to go.

Both directions looked equally unappealing. Both seemed to lead deeper into thickly forested mountains. Neither had so much as a signpost or marker. He realized that he couldn't remember when he'd seen the last human, the last car other than Season's Jeep. He might as well have been in a primeval wilderness. He picked the right fork, because that seemed more of a continuation of the road he was already on, while the left would require actually turning off that road. But after driving that way for about ten minutes, he still hadn't caught sight of the Jeep, and the snow was, if anything, falling faster than before. The road was practically obliterated by it. Even with four-wheel drive, it was treacherously slippery. And if he had picked wrong, then with every passing minute they were getting farther and farther away on the other road, their tracks wiped away by the blizzard.

At a loss for any other options, Scott stopped his vehicle and killed the engine. He stepped out into the snow, listening. The air smelled like pine; falling snowflakes kissed his cheeks and eyelids. He had hoped to hear the roar of Season's Jeep, but there was only utter silence—not a bird, not a distant airplane, not the chirp of a cricket.

He tried Kerry's phone again. No service.

He ducked back inside, got the gun from his backpack. He hated the thing. Aiming for a faraway tree, he threw it as far as he could. It hit some branches and fell through them, crashing to the ground beneath. Snow shaken loose by its passage dropped over it. Then the silence returned, made somehow more absolute than before.

He could have been the last person on Earth.

This was just *perfect*.

Christmas Eve. Taking the new honey to meet the folks for Christmas dinner. And the ex calls and says drop everything, never mind your life, the girl I have the hots for now is in danger.

Ninety percent of the world's females, Brandy figured, would have offered a two-word response. But then, ninety percent of the world's population—more like ninety-nine point nine, probably, with a few more nines thrown in for good measure—were blissfully unaware that beings like Season Howe existed. That knowledge, combined with the belief that Season had targeted their little summer group for extinction, meant that Brandy's reaction would have to be somewhat different than the vast majority's.

Instead of telling him to get lost—or any of the other combinations of two words that came to mind—her answer had to be "I'm coming." It wasn't fair. But then, no one had ordained that life had to be fair. In fact, it often seemed that the better it was going in one area or another, balance decreed that it had to get worse somewhere else.

So: Adam good, Season bad. And as good as Adam was, on the scale Season's badness was far, far worse.

Which meant her response wasn't in doubt. The only question remaining was, how did she tell her parents and Adam that she was going to New Hampshire for Christmas, instead of their house?

Her mom would want her head. Her dad would sulk unpleasantly. DJ, her little brother, would probably threaten bodily harm. The various relatives—aunts, uncles, cousins—who were expected would be overly concerned and offer bits of helpful advice to the family. Of course, she wouldn't be around so she wouldn't have to listen to that part, but she'd get plenty of complaints about it when she got back.

Bright side, she thought, *maybe I'll get killed and won't have to face them at all.*

Not funny, she amended. *Ask Josh and Mace if it's funny.*

Still, there were times when one needed black humor to fend off the real horrors of life, and this was looking like one of those times. If she couldn't make unpleasant jokes about it, she probably couldn't face it at all.

Brandy realized that sitting in her apartment stewing wasn't going to do any good— this was one of those occasions where the sooner she acted, the better. She picked the phone out of her lap and dialed Rebecca's cell.

While she drove through the gathering storm, Season chatted casually about a wide variety of subjects, from clothes to cars, environmental issues to restaurants and resorts all around the world. She was well informed and erudite, and Kerry couldn't help enjoying the conversation.

The only thing Season refused to discuss was what Kerry had wanted to talk about in the first place. "We can talk about all of that, but not here, not in the car," Season had said when Kerry pressed the issue. "When we get where we're going." But she wouldn't tell Kerry where it was they were going, only that it was someplace safe, someplace they wouldn't be disturbed.

Kerry was terrified by the whole idea of going anywhere with Season.

But curiosity outweighed her terror. Season had made some explosive charges at Mother Blessing's place, and Kerry was determined to get to the truth about them. Was Season Mother Blessing's mother and Daniel's grandmother? Who was really responsible for the tragedy at Slocumb, Virginia, in 1704, which had kicked off this whole multicentury war of witches? These were the issues that Kerry was really concerned with, not which European chef made the best chocolate desserts—although chocolate still ranked pretty high on the priority scale.

She rode along beside Season, commenting or asking a question on occasion and answering some about her own earlier life—before San Diego—and found herself surprised at the witch's geniality. The radio played holiday music that made a strange counterpoint to the ride. She didn't relax—that was a leap of faith she wasn't ready to take, not when the woman behind the wheel had the power to end her life with a word or two. But she became somewhat less tense as the drive wore on, at least until the storm blew in and erased visibility down to a few yards. Season expressed full confidence in her Jeep's ability to handle the snowy roads, and Kerry could see that she was a capable driver. *But then*, she thought, *she's had a century of practice, so why not? Probably started out driving a Model T.*

They drove deeper into the wilderness, and Season became less chatty as she had to struggle more with just keeping her wheels on the road—or seeing the road at all. It was still only early afternoon, but the sky was twilight-dark, the world reduced to nothing but snowflakes flickering in the headlights. Looming over everything were the mountains, rounded and stolid, like hunched-over elders quietly disapproving of everything they observed. Kerry knew these mountains were older than the Rockies she had flown over twice, earlier in the year. Those had knife-edged peaks that looked like they could slice open the airplane. But these, while less imposing, were still higher than anything back home in Illinois, or down in the flat mid-Atlantic region.

Finally, when Kerry was starting to worry that they really would become trapped by the ever-thicker downfall, Season pulled off the road onto a barely-there driveway and stopped with her headlights shining on a small wooden cabin nestled in a stand of tall pines. Snow had drifted in front of the cabin's door and piled on its rooftop, but the structure seemed sound enough.

"Here we are," Season announced.

"*Where* we are?"

"Where we're going. Kind of a little hideaway I have."

"I thought you liked being where there were lots of people around," Kerry mentioned. "The whole safety in numbers thing, like with the resorts?"

"I do," Season confirmed. "But I also know that, strategically, sometimes it's important to be able to change the way I do things. Can't be predictable all the time. So I have a few of these kinds of places scattered around the country, for emergency use."

"Are we still in New Hampshire?"

"Yes," Season replied. "I like to keep my hideaways within an hour or so of the resorts I frequent. Weather permitting, of course."

Kerry looked at the weather. "Think we'll be snowed in?"

"Almost definitely," Season said. "We'll be

fine, though. There are plenty of supplies and firewood inside."

"Okay, then. Might as well get to it." She opened the Jeep door and grabbed her duffel from the back seat. "Guess it's going to be a white Christmas for us."

10

The cabin was, in fact, much more impressive inside than out. That seemed to be a habit with witches, Kerry thought, remembering the way Mother Blessing's place in the swamp had looked like a falling-down old trapper's cabin from the outside, but a modern suburban home on the inside.

Witches had other advantages, too. Starting a fire was no problem for Season, who simply laid some logs into a gigantic stone fireplace and ignited them magically. Within minutes the place had already started to warm up, and Kerry was able to shed her coat and look around a little.

The interior reflected the cabin theme from outside, but in a much more luxurious way than Kerry would have guessed from the primitive facade. The walls were knotty pine, but highly polished, warm, and rich looking. The hardwood floor was dotted with beautiful rugs. Season's furniture was rustic but comfortable, all wood, well crafted and padded. A counter or breakfast bar separated the huge main room from a kitchen area with cabinets in the same golden pine as the floors. The place had two bedrooms, and Season showed Kerry which one would be hers—a cozy space with a big wooden bed covered by a lush comforter. The room was tucked under the eaves at the back of the house, timbered ceiling slanting away toward what looked, through the one small window, like unlimited, infinite pine forest.

We really are alone up here, Kerry thought, with a sensation of dread. *Anything could happen. They'd never find my body.*

But if Season had intended to kill her, she could have done so at any time. Why bother bringing her up here, showing her a bedroom, getting towels from a linen closet for her?

No reason that Kerry could determine. Which could only mean that Season hadn't brought her here to kill her, but to talk, as she had insisted.

Well, that was fine. That's what Kerry wanted too. She had hoped to do it nearer civilization, where she could get away if she needed to. But she wasn't the one calling the shots. Since they'd climbed into the Jeep, Season had been, literally as well as figuratively, in the driver's seat.

Season had suggested that Kerry take a shower, and given how nasty she felt, Kerry had happily agreed. She took her towels into the hall bathroom—her own master suite, Season said, had another—and was delighted to find that it was just as deluxe as the rest of the place. The fixtures were gleaming brass, the tub enclosed in sparkling glass. When Kerry undressed and turned on the shower, the water rushed forth steaming hot. Bottles of shampoo, conditioner, and cleanser were lined up on a shelf inside the tub enclosure. Twenty minutes later, showered, having found a brand new toothbrush and a tube of toothpaste lying next to the sink, she felt like a new person. She wrapped her long black hair up in one of the towels, wrapped the other one around herself, and went back across the hall to the bedroom. When she opened the bathroom door, she realized that Season had been busy too—cooking aromas competed with the wood burning in the fireplace, and the smell instantly reminded Kerry of how long it had been since breakfast.

Back in her room she dug a clean pair of sweatpants, a thick green cableknit sweater, and fuzzy white socks from her duffel. After rubbing lotion into her hands, arms, and legs, she dressed quickly. She carried the towels back into the bathroom to hang, tied her hair back, applied a little eyeliner. She could have done more, but she felt more presentable than she had in days, and the smells from the kitchen were making her crazy.

"I hope pasta's okay," Season said when Kerry found her. She had a big pot boiling on the stove. She'd changed into a soft tan turtleneck and faded jeans and wore her hair loose. "It was fast and easy. There's garlic bread, too, and some salad."

"Pasta's fine," Kerry said. She was afraid that she might actually start to drool. "Smells wonderful."

"Thanks," Season said with a smile. "I like to cook, but I don't really get much chance to."

"How did you get fresh salad vegetables here if you haven't been here lately?" Kerry wondered.

Season just laughed.

"Oh," Kerry said, realizing the foolishness of her question. There wasn't much Season couldn't do, apparently—conjuring some fresh lettuce, tomatoes, and cucumbers wouldn't be much of a trick for her.

There was a rough-hewn pine dining table beside the breakfast bar, on which Season had put out thick white linen place mats and heavy pewter tableware. "Can I do anything?" Kerry asked.

"It's just about ready," Season said by way of reply. She picked up the pot with two massive potholders and carried it to the sink, where she dumped it into a colander. "Meat sauce all right with you?"

"Yeah, that's fine," Kerry said. "Thanks for this, by the way. I am just starving."

"Me too." She put the pasta back into the pot and put it back on its burner. On another burner a pot of red sauce simmered noisily. Season poured the red sauce over the pasta, stirring the two together, and let it cook for a couple of minutes. "This makes it so the sauce doesn't just slide off the pasta," she explained. "Holds the heat in, too, so it stays warm longer."

"Works for me," Kerry said. She appreciated the effort, although right at this moment she was less concerned with technique and more with actually eating.

"Can you grab the bread?" Season asked. She was busy stirring the pasta and sauce, so Kerry picked up the potholders and went to the oven. Inside, the crusty garlic bread was just the right shade of golden brown. She drew it out and put it on the cutting board that Season indicated, carrying that to the table and setting it down.

"I think we're ready," Season announced. "What do you want to drink?"

"What is there?" Kerry asked. But at Season's smile, she answered for herself. "Oh, right—everything. I'll have a peach Snapple, I guess."

"It's in the fridge," Season said, putting the pasta into a serving dish. "Help yourself."

Kerry opened the refrigerator. There was indeed a peach Snapple there, on the top shelf.

And nothing else. Kerry took the bottle, leaving the refrigerator empty. She suspected it had not been empty a minute earlier, and probably wasn't now.

So Season had a sense of humor, on top of everything else. That was unexpected, but the kind of surprise—like this lunch—that Kerry could use more of.

After they had eaten—both largely silent, more interested in consuming than conversing—Kerry cleared the dishes and they retired to the living room to sit by the fire. Outside, night had fallen, but snowflakes continued to drop past the light from the cabin's windows. Season took a glass of red wine in and sat on the rug in front of the fireplace, setting her glass down on the hearth. She carried in a bowl of mixed nuts and a plate of cookies and put them on a coffee table. Kerry brewed some orange pekoe tea and joined her, taking a seat on a cushy couch. Season watched her get comfortable, a serious expression on her lovely face. She chewed a little on her lower lip, which Kerry found surprisingly girlish for someone as old as Season was.

Then again, if you get right down to it, walking and breathing are pretty girlish for someone as old as her. Especially if she's really Daniel's grandmother.

After a minute Season broke the silence. "You've got some questions, Kerry," she said. "Not all at once, please. And I reserve the right not to answer everything right away. I'm tired, and I don't want to talk all evening."

This presented Kerry with a quandary. How would she know which questions to ask and which to avoid? There was so much she wanted to know—not just about the areas in which Season and Mother Blessing contradicted each other, but about Season's long war with Daniel, and about her powers and abilities. She was still furious at Season, but the long day with her had exposed a human side that she had never expected to find, and that tempered her rage somewhat. Season may have been a monster, but she wasn't all monster, all the time.

"Start at the beginning, then," she said finally. "What happened that day in Slocumb?"

Season shook her head. "Not tonight," she replied. "That story's too long for now. Next?"

Most of Kerry's questions were going to involve long, complex answers, she figured. She hoped Season wouldn't try to dodge them all. "Okay," she said after coming up with a different approach. "The way I see it, you killed three of my friends, Daniel Blessing, Mace Winston, and Josh Quinn. And poor old Edgar Brandvold. How can you justify murder?"

Season took a sip of wine and studied Kerry with her deep blue eyes. "Murder has been justified in human society since the first caveman clobbered another one over the head with a stick," she said. "But you're not here for a civics lesson, so I'll take them one at a time.

"Yes, I killed Daniel. From your reaction at the time, and some things you've said and done since then, I take it he meant something to you."

"We were in love," Kerry said quietly. She didn't want to start talking about that, didn't want to shed any tears for him in front of his murderer.

"I thought it was something like that. For your sake, I'm sorry. For my own, though—he had been chasing me for centuries, Kerry. We've battled many times, done some damage, but there was never anything final. Never a conclusion. I was tired of running, tired of having to look over my shoulder, of never sitting still or trusting anyone. And he was never going to let up."

"That's true."

"And I shouldn't need to remind you, Kerry, that when it happened, he attacked me. You were there. You saw it all. He hit me with everything he had, thought he had killed me. And I was hurt, bad. Just not as hurt as he believed."

Kerry remembered the day vividly, especially in her nightmares. It had happened just as Season described. They had trapped Season in her rented house—Daniel, Kerry, Brandy, Scott, Rebecca, and Josh—and lured her outside, where Daniel had unleashed a barrage of magical attacks against her. As Season said, she had gone down. Even Kerry thought she was finished. But from somewhere, she had summoned an unexpected reserve of strength. With Daniel's guard down she had been able to claim the advantage, and she had bested him, while Kerry and her friends looked on in horror.

"Okay, yeah," Kerry admitted. "That's true. But—"

"There are no buts, Kerry," Season said. "He would not have just given up. There was no talking to him, no rational discussion. He wanted me dead, and he wanted it to happen before the next Witches' Convocation. You know what that is?"

Mother Blessing had told Kerry about the Convocation, a gathering of witches held every five hundred years to discuss problems and techniques and to try witches accused of crimes. "Yes."

"If I thought he would let up, if he would have let me live until the Convocation, where I could have taken some legal action, that would have been fine. Obviously, I've spent the last few hundred years running and hiding, trying to avoid violence, instead of seeking him out and just finishing it off. But the closer we got to the Convocation, the more he came after me. Finally, I'd had enough. At that moment, with all of you there, he almost got me, and I did what I had to do."

Kerry didn't want to admit there was any truth at all in what Season was saying. She wanted to hold onto her anger, to wave it like a flag. Whatever the circumstances, Season had been the one who struck a fatal blow, not Daniel.

She knew, however, that Daniel would have if he'd been able. His intention had been to kill Season or die trying. She had simply held the better hand, or played her cards more skillfully. Either way, Season's version of things rang true.

"It happened more or less like that with Abraham, too—Daniel's brother. Have you heard about him?"

"Daniel said they ambushed you in your room," Kerry told her.

"That's right. And killed my lover. I fought back hard. I killed Abraham, and thought I had killed Daniel then too." She took another sip of wine and looked away from Kerry. "My life would have been a lot simpler if I'd made sure."

"What about Mace?" Kerry asked. "What threat was he to you?"

Season glanced up again. "I don't know the name. He was the one with the big blue car?"

"That was Suzie," Kerry replied. She was still stuffed from the meal, but she took a couple of nuts and nibbled on them. "The car,

I mean. Yes, Mace had a big blue Lincoln."

"Yes. That one might have been avoidable," Season admitted. "I knew I had injured Daniel, but he'd escaped before I could finish him. I thought if I could track him down quickly enough, before he had healed . . . I could end things that much sooner. But he had come into contact with you and your friends, somehow, and he was screening you all from me. When that one—Mace, you said?"

"Right, Mace Winston. Kind of a hick, but sweet, you know?"

Season nodded, biting a cookie. "When he left your group, he suddenly came onto my radar. That's a metaphor, by the way—not real radar. So I interrupted his escape to question him about where Daniel might be found. He tried to resist. I admit that I overreacted. I didn't mean to kill him, but I did. I'm terribly sorry for that."

"Not so sorry that you didn't kill Josh, too."

Season looked confused. "I'm sorry? You mentioned that name before, too. I don't know who you mean."

"Oh, come on," Kerry said, anger simmering

to the surface again. "Josh. Palefaced Goth boy, Las Vegas. Do you kill so many people you can't remember them all?"

Season put her wineglass down and pointed a finger at Kerry. "Oh, now I know who you're talking about. I was there when he died, but I didn't kill him."

"He wrote your name in his own blood on the side of a slot machine," Kerry said.

"I didn't know that," Season admitted. "But it doesn't change anything. Maybe he wrote it because he recognized me, or because I was the last person to speak to him."

"Because you killed him."

"I didn't, Kerry," Season insisted. "I've admitted to the ones I did, even Mace, which was accidental. Why would I lie about this one?"

"Why did you talk to him, then?" Kerry pressed.

"He helped me, or tried to. A couple of Mother Blessing's simulacra were attacking me in the casino. He stepped in front of them, slowed them down. It was like—like he was trying to reason with them. You know simulacra?"

"I've met a few."

"Reasoning isn't their forte," Season understated. "If he was one of your friends, I would have thought he'd have been egging them on."

"He knew we were coming. We were in the parking structure, I think, when it happened. Or almost there. Maybe he wanted them to hold off until we arrived so we could all attack you together."

Season shrugged. "Perhaps. All I know is that the simulacra didn't react well to being thwarted. They removed your friend from their path the only way they knew how. After I dispatched them, I checked on him—on Josh—but it was too late. He was already fading. And casino security was on the way. I made him comfortable in his last moments, so at least he wouldn't be in pain, and I left."

Kerry found herself wanting to believe that, even though she didn't know if she should. But she liked the idea that Josh's death had been without pain.

"You said one other name, earlier," Season reminded her.

Daniel, Mace, Josh, Kerry thought. Those were the deaths she had carried around inside her for so long, the reasons she had wanted Season Howe dead. Then it came back to her. "Oh, yeah. Edgar Brandvold. Down in Wallaceton, Virginia. Outside the swamp."

"Oh, right," Season said. "A longtime ally of Mother Blessing's."

"He did her favors from time to time," Kerry countered. "Brought her groceries, that kind of thing."

"More than that," Season said. "He was a kind of early warning system for her. She'd taught him a few tricks, and he patrolled the eastern border of the swamp to make sure her privacy wasn't compromised. When I found him, he cast a spell, tried to tear my head off. But I've got pretty good reflexes. I dodged and counterattacked. His reflexes weren't so good."

"His walking stick was driven through his heart."

"A girl's gotta do what a girl's gotta do. It was a walking stick when you saw it. It was a serpent before that, with a mouth the size of a car door, trying to chomp on me."

The story sounded just ridiculous enough to be true. And Kerry had seen equally bizarre things. She had wondered why Season had killed Edgar—the man seemed ancient and frail, like he couldn't possibly have been a threat. It seemed clearer now.

"Okay, I guess I can buy that. So then, what—"

Season held up a hand to stop her. "That's enough for one night," she said. "I'm beat. Driving through that snow really took a lot out of me. And it's early enough that I can shower and get a good night's sleep. Let's turn in now, and we can talk more tomorrow."

"But—"

"If we don't go to sleep," Season cautioned, "then Santa Claus won't come."

"There isn't even a tree," Kerry pointed out. "Somehow, I doubt that Santa is going to visit this place. There aren't any good little girls here anyway."

"You might be surprised," Season said. "Never count the old guy out." She stood up and took the dirty dishes to the kitchen. "Tomorrow!" she called back over her shoulder.

"Okay," Kerry said. "But tomorrow, everything's fair game."

"I promise."

And I'm going to hold you to that, Season, Kerry thought. *That's a promise you won't get out of.*

11

All righty, then.

It wouldn't be fair, I guess, to say that twenty-four hours ago I had been ready to kill Season Howe on sight. I had already decided at that point that I wanted to talk to her first, to try to get some things straight in my own mind. I wanted a clearer picture of what it was I had become involved in.

Then I would kill her.

And now . . .

Is it called the Stockholm Syndrome? Something like that. Wherein kidnap victims begin to identify with their captors, sometimes even helping protect them from the police. Although it's not fair, probably, to say that someone going, "Hey, let's take a ride so we can talk," and the other someone going, "Okay," is the same as being kidnapped.

She's not exactly holding me here against my will. Except it's not like I could leave, at least not easily, given that we are a million miles from civilization and I have no actual idea of where.

But I came willingly, and I don't feel like I'm in real danger from her. That could change. I'm not sure I'll sleep all that soundly tonight, and it has nothing to do with listening for reindeer hooves on the roof. But I don't think she'd have fed me and talked to me about having killed Daniel, and Mace, and Edgar, but not Josh, if she was just going to turn around and kill me.

I'm not sure, in fact, why she brought me here, why she agreed to tell me all this. Maybe that's something she'll reveal tomorrow.

That would be good, because I could sure use a clue here. Once again I'm feeling kind of out in the wilderness without a map, which is not only literally true but metaphorically as well. I still don't know what happened in Slocumb, but if Season is to be believed, then Mother Blessing, not Season, is really responsible for Josh's death. And Mother Blessing knew, when I got back to her place from Las Vegas, that I was devastated by what had happened there.

So why would she continue to let me think Season was responsible, if she knew full well that she wasn't? That would be . . .

Hello! Clue much? If she wanted some proxy stand-in to take over the hunt for Season when Daniel was gone, what better way to keep that person interested than throwing the body of a friend or two down and letting her think Season had done it?

And once again, Kerry the slow-witted comes to realize there's much more to Mother Blessing than meets the eye. And none of it good.

So tonight. Kind of strange, sitting around with the killer of the man I loved, sharing cookies and nuts, drinking and talking. And underneath it all— also kind of strange—feeling like, hey, I'm glad I haven't killed her, because she's kind of neat.

"Kind of neat." Too old-fashioned? Kind of rad, maybe. Kind of phat. Whatever, it's Christmas Eve, and if there is ever a time when old-fashioned is apropos, this is it. "Apropos," also old-fashioned, methinks.

And "methinks," again also.

Methinks I'm dodging the central issue here, which has to do with not killing Season after all. But she makes a kind of sense that I am having a hard time disregarding. Yes, she killed Daniel, and I hate her for that. But she's right; he was trying to kill her. I really thought he had killed her. She was so brutalized, so still—I thought she was dead, and so did he. But she wasn't, and then he was, and it was just about that fast.

And tonight, when she was talking about the necessity of killing him, and Abraham, she was looking right at me, flat and level, letting me see that she was telling me the truth. But then she turned away. Not like someone who was lying might, but . . . when she turned back, it looked like there might have been a tear in her eye.

A trick? Too much wine? Anything's possible, right? But the fact is, it looked like talking about their deaths choked her up.

Like, maybe, a grandmother would cry when talking about the deaths of her grandsons.

Sleep on that, Kerry Profitt.

It's almost midnight. Merry Christmas.

K.

"Merry Christmas!"

After coming down off the mountain, Scott had paid higher-than-premium fare for a short-term condo rental near Berlin, New Hampshire, offering enough to make the people who had really rented it happy to go bunk with friends, knowing that their ski holiday had netted them a significant profit. But he had figured they'd need a base of operations if they were going to have any hope of finding Kerry.

"They" came at seven o'clock on Christmas morning. Scott woke to their insistent ringing. Bleary-eyed, he pawed for his glasses. He had slept poorly, worrying about Kerry, but a couple of hours ago had finally drifted off. Then the doorbell started in. On the way out of the bedroom he caught a glimpse of himself in the mirror—bed-head sent his brown hair shooting off in every direction at once. He had slept in a T-shirt and boxers, so he tugged on yesterday's jeans, then opened the door for Brandy and Rebecca, who, in spite of having been on the road for hours and hours, both looked at least ten times more awake than he felt. They entered with holiday greetings at least twenty times more cheerful than he could return, given the circumstances.

"Hey, you guys," he said. Brandy accepted a quick hug, even returning it with a couple of friendly pats on the back. Her familiar, slightly fruity scent brought a rush of emotion flooding into him, even more than the sight and feel of her did.

"Did we wake you?"

"Well, it's either that or I always look this bad," Scott said. "I'll hope for the former."

Brandy shook off her vintage fake-fur-lined coat and handed it to Scott. Fortunately, the place had come with a standing coat rack, so he didn't have to try to figure out someplace to put it. "You don't look—well, okay, yes you do. You look awful. You want to get some more sleep?"

He turned to Rebecca, who squeezed him tighter than Brandy had. "Don't listen to her," Rebecca said. "Anyone has a right to look like they spent the night under a bus if they want to."

"Gee, thanks, Beck," Scott said, stifling a yawn. "I'll make coffee. You want some?"

Brandy shook her head. Underneath her coat she wore a red wool turtleneck and brown denim pants. Her hair was tightly braided and lay close to her scalp. "Caffeine is what got us here. I think we sampled every energy drink on the market. I have any more,

I'll start bouncing off your walls. Which, by the way, nice place. How'd you score it?"

"Found someone willing to accept a wheelbarrow full of cash. Don't tell the land-lord, because he doesn't know."

Brandy smiled. "You're becoming very resourceful, Scott," she said. "Good job."

"Definitely," Rebecca added. She doffed her puffy blue ski coat, revealing a gray UC Santa Cruz sweatshirt with pink corduroy pants and black lace-up pleather boots.

"You don't know the half of it." He was thinking of the gun he'd acquired. That had been resourceful. *And stupid,* he added.

"I'm sure not." Brandy went into the living room, furnished in Modern Rental oaks and earth tones, and took a seat on a sofa.

"Have a seat," he said, after the fact.

"Thanks," Rebecca replied. *Other people are always more polite than exes,* Scott observed. He crossed through the living room into the condo's kitchenette to start the coffee. He needed a jolt, even if no one else did.

"What do we do now?" Brandy asked. "Is there a plan?"

Scott was suddenly, unreasonably infuriated

by her. "I don't know, Brandy! I don't have a plan. All I know is that Kerry is out there somewhere, that Season's got her, and we have to find them!"

Brandy got up off the sofa, putting her hands out. "Whoa, Scott. I know you're frantic over this. I am too, believe me. But let's keep our eye on the real problem, okay? Don't take your frustrations out on me."

"Yeah, I'm sorry, Brandy," he said, deflated just as quickly as he had blown up. She was right, he wasn't mad at her. He was just mad.

"I was looking at a New Hampshire map on the way here," Brandy pointed out. "And there must be, like, thousands of square miles of wilderness up here."

"Probably," he agreed glumly. He went into the kitchen and stared at the coffee, willing it to brew faster. He was either going to have to go back to bed or down the whole pot, and Brandy seemed intent on talking.

"So how are we going to—"

"Brandy!" he interrupted, unable to keep his emotions in check. "I just said I don't have a plan, okay? I don't know how we're going to find her! I just know that we have to—that if we don't,

Season's going to kill her! That's what she does."

"Okay, you guys," Rebecca said, obviously uneasy with their arguing. "We'll figure something out. Or she'll get in touch with us. Have you tried her phone lately?"

"I tried it all day and night yesterday. She's out of range, or else she has it turned off."

"That'll make things tougher," Brandy pointed out. "But there's got to be a way. You know where you lost them, right?"

"Yeah, basically," Scott replied. He poured ground coffee into a filter and stuck it in the coffeemaker. "But it was snowing like crazy. I'm pretty sure I can find it again, but there are no tracks or anything."

"But maybe we can come up with some kind of organized search pattern," Rebecca suggested. "Mark off a grid and take it section by section."

"We'd have to have snowmobiles for that," Scott countered. "It's really wilderness up there—not many roads, lots of open country and forest."

"But they were in a car of some kind," Brandy said. "So there must be a way to get to where they are on roads."

"They were in a Jeep," Scott answered. "They were sticking to roads as far as I saw, but it's possible that they didn't have to. They could have taken some little dirt road, or even left the roads altogether."

"You still have the RAV4, right?" Rebecca asked him.

"Yeah," he said. "It's got four-wheel drive, but it's not the off-roader the Jeep is. They could definitely get to places I can't."

"Okay," Brandy said. "But at least it gives us a place to start. And if we get going soon, we'll have a full day of light. The longer we sit around here the less time we'll have to search."

That was true, Scott knew. But the coffee-maker was just beginning to fill the pot. He had not had enough sleep to function at his best all day. While he knew that caffeine was no substitute for sleep, it looked like it was the best he was going to get.

Rebecca had gone almost immediately to Grand Central Station upon receiving the anxious call from Brandy. She had been expecting it ever since Kerry had taken off for New Hampshire. Kerry was brave and smart, but she wouldn't be able to cope with Season all by herself. It had been stupid of Rebecca to let her go off and try. She had hoped that Kerry could keep Scott out of trouble, but now it seemed she was in danger herself. That knowledge was the only reason Rebecca had been willing to come, to risk facing Season again. Kerry should have gathered them all from the beginning— not that there was much the rest of them could have done that Kerry couldn't, but at least they'd have been together. Taking them one by one seemed to be Season's standard procedure, and they couldn't let her continue to do that.

Her parents had been upset, but not outrageously so. Their holiday was over anyway. She had been on a train within an hour. Four hours after that—four hours of increasing anxiety, mingled with some outright terror—she was in Boston.

Brandy met her at the train station looking terrible—her eyes bloodshot and puffy, the skin under her nose raw. She had obviously been crying.

Once they were settled in the car, heading out of town, she had asked Brandy what was wrong.

"It's just . . . this whole thing stinks," Brandy answered. "I'm seeing this great new guy—his name is Adam, you'd love him, Rebecca. Really, you would. Anyway, things have been moving kind of fast, and it seems like we're pretty serious about each other. He was going to go with me to my folks' house for Christmas dinner. We were both super nervous about it, but I was looking forward to it too, because Adam is really mature and charming and everything. He would have blown Mom away.

"But then, you know, Scott had to go all *America's Most Wanted* on us."

Rebecca was shocked. "Brandy! It's not like he made Season take her."

"No, I know," Brandy admitted. "I don't mean to make light of it. Kerry's in trouble and we've got to be there for her, just like she would be for us. It's just—the timing was incredibly sucky. I told Adam I had to cancel, and he was all pouty and sad. I think it would have been better if he'd been mad, but he wasn't. He was just, 'Okay, if that's what you really want to do.' Which, of course, it's not. But it's what I have to do, and he didn't seem to get that."

"What did your parents say?" Rebecca asked.

Brandy concentrated on her driving for a minute. Rebecca figured she was probably trying to compose a response. "Let's just say they weren't happy," she said finally. "Mom just about blew a gasket. 'I've been cooking for three days! Everyone's expecting to see you, and to meet Adam! What do you mean, you have to go?' That kind of thing. DJ thought it was Adam's fault somehow and offered to break his legs."

"You tell him to break Season's instead?"

"If I dared to tell him about Season, he'd try it. And of course she'd fry him."

"Like she'll do to us if she gets a chance."

"Well, yeah," Brandy agreed. "Anyway, there was a scene. Mom shrieking, Dad kind of humphing, DJ storming around hitting things. It wasn't pretty."

"Doesn't sound like it."

Rebecca was glad to be with Brandy, happy to see her friend in spite of the unpleasant reason for the reunion. Conversation drifted to less emotionally charged topics as the miles melted away behind them. The farther north they went, the worse the weather grew, until what should have been a four-hour drive turned into eight. Christmas carols and caffeine helped them stay alert and on the road, but even those things couldn't help stave off the very real horror Rebecca felt as they got closer to where Season had last been seen. Rebecca worried about Kerry, but she worried about herself and the others, too.

And now they were here, in Scott's emergency rental. And Kerry, the reason for their hurried trip, was somewhere out there.

12

Kerry slept better than she'd expected—
better than I had a right to, under the circumstances,
she thought—and when she got up in the
morning, donning the fuzzy terrycloth robe
that hung on the back of her bedroom door,
Season was already busy in the kitchen. The
cabin smelled like bacon and garlic, which were
both happy aromas as far as she was concerned.

"Merry Christmas," Season said when she
saw her. She wore a white sweater with a red
reindeer shape on it and black pants.

"Merry Christmas," Kerry echoed. "That
smells great."

"I hope you're hungry," Season said.
"There are omelets, garlic home fries, bacon,
and juice. And I made a pot of Earl Grey."

"Mmm," Kerry said. "Sounds wonderful."

"Well, you were right. Santa didn't find us. So I figured we could eat our sorrows away."

"I'm in favor of that idea." Kerry still felt strange, socializing like this with Season. But she had slept all night under the witch's roof, and she had not been attacked. She was still here, still in one piece. The more she got to know Season, the more she believed that they had all been wrong about her. Not completely wrong, since she had admitted to killing Mace and Daniel. But wrong in some very significant ways nonetheless.

A few minutes later Season had dished up breakfast, and Kerry sat across from her at the table. The food tasted delicious—Season could become a chef, if she ever decided to give up the witch gig.

They ate in relative silence, Kerry realizing with the first few mouthfuls how truly ravenous she was. After they were done and Kerry was washing dishes, Season made her an offer.

"For your Christmas present," she said, "I'll answer ten questions for you."

"Just ten?" Kerry replied.

"Choose carefully," Season admonished with a smile. "Now you're down to nine."

"Oh, jeez," Kerry said. "It's going to be like that? That wasn't a question, so don't count it."

"Whenever you're ready," Season said. "Have you looked outside? We're not going anywhere today, so I'm not in any hurry."

Kerry hadn't, but she wasn't surprised. The way the snow had still been coming down when she'd gone to bed, she would have been amazed if any of the roads they took here had still been passable.

Nine questions, though. And she had to be careful how she phrased them, obviously. It wouldn't do to waste another one.

She finished washing out the last pan and pulled a towel from its hook to begin drying. "Okay," she said. "Here goes. Is Mother Blessing your real daughter?"

Season looked directly at her. "Yes," she said simply.

"I hope that's not all the elaboration I get," Kerry said, careful to phrase it as a statement.

"I'm not trying to be difficult, Kerry," Season said. "But there are rules about this kind of thing. And before you spend a question asking what kind of thing I mean, I'll just tell you: Witches aren't supposed to give non-witches unnecessary information about our kind."

"But I am—I mean, I'm becoming a witch. Mother Blessing was teaching me. She said you didn't have to be born a witch, but you could be trained."

"And she was right. That's the only reason I'm giving you this chance now. If you were completely non-witch, you wouldn't even get this much. Daniel broke more rules than you'll ever know when he told you everything he did. Had he survived until the Convocation, he'd have been severely disciplined."

"Well, I think that sucks," Kerry said. "He loved me, and he wanted to protect me."

"I didn't say that I thought he did anything wrong," Season said. "Only that he broke the rules. I'm trying to be more careful. But I won't leave you with just yes or no answers. Yes, she is my daughter. She wasn't always, as you might guess, called Mother Blessing. When she was born, her father and I called her Myrtle. It was traditional in those days for the children of witches to have names from nature."

She stopped, and Kerry guessed that meant the answer was complete. She was going to have to be very careful, with just eight questions remaining. She could jump around, asking the first things that came to mind. But that would probably be a good way of ensuring that when they were done, big holes in her understanding remained. She had to play it smarter to make sure she got the whole story.

With the last of the dishes dried, she came out from behind the kitchen counter. She still hadn't dressed, but it was a lazy Christmas Day and she didn't care. The fuzzy robe kept her warm and comfortable. "Let's sit down," she suggested.

Season followed her to the living room. As on the night before, a fire crackled in the fireplace, giving the room a homey, pleasant feel. Kerry sat in a soft chair while Season stretched out on the couch.

"Who was Mother Blessing's father, then?" she asked.

"His name was Forest. We married young—but then, everyone did in those days. That was in 1649, in England. Charles I was beheaded, Charles II crowned, and I was married, all in the same year. It was an eventful time."

"Sounds like it."

"Anyway, Forest and I had many good years together. We moved to the colonies, where it seemed there was more freedom, and we were less likely to be hanged for witchcraft. I was pregnant before I learned that Forest was, in fact, evil—he had been hiding it well, but not well enough, as it turned out. I left him and moved to Slocumb with young Myrtle, my only child. We were happy there, for a while, and the people came to accept my skills, seeking my help when they needed something I could provide.

"But Myrtle, as it happened, inherited her father's nature, not mine. Evil can only be repressed for so long; eventually it reveals itself. The same happened, sadly, with Myrtle. I think having a child herself set it off."

A child? Kerry wondered. She had only ever heard about Daniel and Abraham—twins, and born after Slocumb's demise. She had to ask.

"What happened to that child?"

"I think I want more tea," Season said instead of answering. "How about you?"

"No, I'm fine," Kerry replied.

Season went into the kitchen, and came back a moment later with a steaming mug. "Sorry," she said. "All this talking makes my throat dry."

"That's okay," Kerry assured her.

"You wanted to know what became of my first grandson. That's part of a longer story. The easy answer is, he died, but you want more than that. I won't count that one, but find another way to ask."

Kerry thought that over. That question had almost been wasted, because she had been suckered into rushing it. She didn't want to do that again. After a minute, she had figured out how to phrase it. "What was the progression of events that led to the destruction of Slocumb?"

Season smiled, and Kerry felt like a student who has come up with the correct answer to a tough problem. "Are you comfortable, Kerry?" she asked. "Don't have to go to the bathroom or anything? Because this one might need a long answer."

Kerry performed a quick mental diagnosis. "I'm fine," she said. "Go ahead."

"All right." Season sipped her tea and smiled again. "Well done, by the way."

"Thanks."

"As I said, Myrtle and I lived in Slocumb. She grew to adulthood there, married a man named Winthrop Blessing—a useless man, I'm afraid, of small mind and scant courage—and had a child of her own. Again, I think it was that event that somehow brought out her dark side. I had been well liked in Slocumb, and Myrtle had been too, until then.

"But she was her father's daughter, after all. Things began to happen in Slocumb, sinister things. Children disappearing, or dying young. Crops failing. Lights appearing in the swamp, leading hunters to their deaths. Animals going rogue, terrorizing the townsfolk.

"I should have known it was her, should have been able to stop it. But I was blinded, I guess. She was my daughter, and even though we had been estranged by that time, I still couldn't bring myself to suspect anything like that. Besides, it had been a long time since I had known Forest, so I guess I had forgotten just how horrible some witches could be.

"What I didn't know was that Forest had come to town. Somehow he heard that he had a grandson—Darius, she had called him, having already abandoned the tradition of naming children from nature and begun to express her perverse irony by choosing biblical names—and he wanted to see the boy. So he sought Myrtle out—or Mother Blessing, as she called herself by then. He didn't tell me he was there, gave me no indication that he had come to visit. But when he and Myrtle got together, they fed one another's madness."

Season paused for a minute. She was staring into space as she talked, with a complete lack of self-consciousness. Kerry thought Season was remembering too deeply, the pain of long-ago events drawing itself clearly on her face.

"If you want to finish this later . . ." Kerry offered.

But Season shook her head. "No, I'm sorry. I'll keep going. There was an—an incident. A widow with three young children woke one morning to find all three children dead, horribly, brutally slaughtered in their beds. Wolf tracks were seen outside in a light snow that had fallen, although no one believed that a wolf had climbed in through a window and silently murdered three children.

"The whole town was up in arms. Some blamed me, some blamed Mother Blessing. I knew it must have been her, of course. But by that point, nobody wanted to listen to reason. They wanted all witches gone, or better yet, dead, and they set out to make that happen.

"Cornered, Mother Blessing and Forest fought back, hard. I did too—fighting for my own life. The town, not that big to begin with, became a magical battleground where no one was safe. Before it was all over, the townspeople had killed Forest and Darius. Mother Blessing's response to that—to two deaths she had prompted in the first place—was to go mad, to level the whole town.

"I tried to stop her, but she was beyond control at that point, her fury having made her a wild woman. And then, to top it off, when the town was a smoking ruin and people from other towns nearby came to offer help, she blamed me. I had been injured in the battle, could barely defend myself, and suddenly they were raising a virtual army against me, going town to town to recruit able-bodied men willing to chase me into the swamp.

"So I did the only thing I could do. I ran.

My grandson, my former husband, my daughter's husband, had all died, and I was made to run like a coward. I found out later that not only did my daughter tell the locals that I was responsible for the devastation in Slocumb, but she went to every witch she could find and spread the same story. Her version of things has become the accepted wisdom, while I've never had a chance to tell mine. Not in any official way, at least."

Kerry sat silently when Season was done, taking it all in. It was much like the story that Mother Blessing had told Daniel, which Kerry had read in his journal. But it was unlike it in other ways, important ways. Ways that rang true to her. In Daniel's version, Mother Blessing had escaped the town before the worst of the destruction began, but still somehow managed to know what had happened, point by point. Season admitted to having stayed through the worst of it, only to leave after the fact when she was blamed for her daughter's crimes.

"I guess I'll have some of that tea now," Kerry said after a little while.

"Do you believe me?" Season asked her.

"I still don't know what to believe," Kerry admitted. She went into the kitchen for some of Season's Earl Grey. In a small microwave oven, she heated a cup. "But what you say makes sense, I think. I'm surprised Daniel never said anything about there being another brother."

"I doubt if she ever told him," Season said. "By the time he was born, she had cemented her story. I was responsible. If she brought Forest and Darius into it, that might have muddied the waters."

"I guess that's true," Kerry said, sitting back down with her tea. "We can take a break if you want."

"I'm okay," Season said. "Thanks for offering, but let's just keep going."

"All right," Kerry said. *Glutton for punishment,* she thought. If this had been her playing true confessions—not that she had much to confess—she'd have been ready for a time-out. But she had thought of her next question, one to which she already had Mother Blessing's answer. "What happens next, in terms of Slocumb? I understand the Witches' Convocation is coming up."

"That's correct," Season said. "Next spring.

There I'll finally get a chance to tell my side of the story, and Mother Blessing will tell hers. It'll be a fair hearing, the first one there's been. One of us will be acquitted and the other will have to pay some penalty.

"But there are more important things at stake here. I doubt that Mother Blessing talks about this much, because she's on the wrong side of it. There is a balance of power in the world, an eternal struggle between order and chaos. Mostly these are natural forces at play. Nature has a tendency toward entropy, but at the same time, its designs are magnificently detailed and precise. Think of a forest left completely on its own—trees grow, trees fall, the underbrush goes wild, until the whole place is completely chaotic—you could never find your way through it. But at the same time, think about the complicated interrelationship between species that allows the forest to grow. Think about the precision with which you can measure the age of the tree by counting its rings. The struggle never ends.

"But witches can help push it toward their preferred way. I try to battle for order. Even my garden, when I had the time and opportunity to grow one, was structured, arranged formally, weeded and tended on a daily basis. No over-grown forest for me.

"Mother Blessing and her sons have kept me on the run so much, though, that I haven't had much time to pull my weight. The scales are tipping—slowly at first, but now faster and faster—toward chaos. If she keeps me from making my contribution—or worse, if she can go to the Convocation and have my powers stripped—then it'll be very hard to stop her from getting her way. Every witch must play his or her part in the balance, and without me in the mix, our side is losing.

"So the Convocation is terribly important, for a number of reasons. But just as important, Mother Blessing can't be allowed to keep me out of action. Things have become too unstable, too desperate."

Kerry wasn't quite sure how to respond to that. It was a whole new and unexpected level. Season was right—Mother Blessing had never given the slightest indication that the stakes were so high. Kerry had been led to believe that, while there might be lives at stake, they were primarily those of witches and of people who had accidentally been drawn into their battles. But now Season's talk of order and chaos made it seem like those few lives were just the tip of the proverbial iceberg, and many, many more might hang in the balance.

"Now I need a break," Kerry said. "That's a lot to take in."

"I know," Season agreed. "I would have broken it to you in an easier way if I could have, but you have to have all the data if you're going to understand it."

"Well, I'm feeling pretty data-rich at this point. I'd like to knock off for a while. Maybe a soak in the tub would help me absorb some of this."

"Sure, no problem," Season said. "You've still got five questions to go."

13

Scott drove Rebecca and Brandy back up to the point where he'd lost Season and Kerry. Snow had covered the little side road, as he had thought, but it had stopped falling, at least for a while, and a heavy gray sky sat atop the peaks as if tethered to them. In four-wheel drive he was able to get up the road to where it forked. From there both roads were buried under drifts—a formless expanse of white spreading in every direction, with trees and snow-topped mountains as background.

"This is where I don't know which way they went," he explained. "I tried one direction for a while, but the snow was falling so heavily I was afraid I'd get stuck. I worked my way back down the hill, and that's when I went into town."

"But that was late yesterday," Brandy observed. "So we don't know if they're still in this area. Or if this was just a back road they took up into Canada or something."

"That's true," Scott admitted.

"Which means we could drive around up here for days, looking for all kinds of side tracks off into the mountains," Rebecca said, "and still never get close to them."

"That's what I'm thinking," Brandy said. "Maybe if we had a helicopter or, I don't know, a spy satellite or something, then this would be a reasonable way to search for them. But without that, this is really a wild goose chase."

Scott stopped the SUV and gripped the wheel, looking glumly at Brandy in the passenger seat. "I told you I didn't have a plan."

"I know," Brandy said mockingly. "And I fully expected that from you."

He made a face at her. "Don't start, Brandy . . ."

"Don't either of you start," Rebecca wailed. "I hate it that you're not together, and if you guys argue I'm just going to cry."

"Crying's not going to help," Scott said. "I should know. I thought I was going to bawl like an infant yesterday when I lost them."

"Because that would have been so manly?"

"Brandy!" Rebecca poked her in the shoulder. Scott caught the motion, and Brandy's wince, out of the corner of his eye and felt secretly glad. Rebecca may not have been on his side, but she wasn't going to sit idly by and let Brandy torment him either.

"So, Mrs. Einstein, do you have any better ideas?" he asked.

If Brandy felt insulted by the nickname, she didn't show it. "We're here now," she replied. "We might as well make the effort. If you couldn't travel much farther, maybe they couldn't either—or maybe they didn't have to. They might be just around the corner."

Scott looked at the snow, the trees. "If there were any corners."

"It's a figurative corner," Brandy shot back. "Like the figurative corners on your block-head."

"If you guys don't quit it, I'm going to get out and walk," Rebecca threatened.

"That'd probably be a better way to find them," Brandy opined. "More likely to see their tracks than from a car."

"But also cold," Scott added.

"There is that," Rebecca agreed. "And with my delicate constitution, not to mention thin blood from all that time in California, maybe I'd better not. So you guys just chill out."

"I'm sorry, Rebecca," Brandy said, turning in her seat to regard their friend. "I guess there's a little leftover tension here, and we're trying to defuse it in a, sort of, you know, good-natured way."

Scott couldn't restrain a bitter laugh. "A *little* tension?"

Brandy turned back to him. "We're riding in a car together and we haven't pulled out any sharp objects," she said. "I'd call that pretty minor."

"Could we, maybe, start looking for Kerry?" Rebecca pleaded. "This is worse than being with you both when all you wanted to do was make out."

Scott remembered those days fondly. He still cared about Brandy—probably still loved her, if he let himself accept the truth. But he knew now that he loved Kerry more. If anything happened to her—if, by his reluctance to interfere yesterday when he'd seen Season leading her away, she was injured or killed—he didn't know how he would live with himself. He guessed that he would be like Kerry had been when Season killed Daniel—driven by lust for revenge. And next time, when he had Season in his sights he wouldn't back down, wouldn't allow himself to be afraid. He was already regretting having thrown that gun away. No way to find it, not before the spring thaw, and by then, he guessed, the moisture would have ruined it.

But he couldn't let himself think like that for more than a couple of moments, or he'd be drawn into a spiral of despondency. Kerry was safe, she was alive, and he would find her before anything bad happened. He *had* to.

He put the RAV4 into low gear and felt its tires slip a little before they bit through the snow to grip the road. This time he took the left fork that he had ignored before. "We're going this way," he announced, hoping to change the subject away from the uncomfortable topic of him and Brandy. "Keep your eyes peeled for any sign of them."

"I always wondered about that phrase,"

Rebecca said. "Is that peeling your eyes like they were grapes? Peeling grapes is hard, and I'm not sure it would actually help you see better."

"I think the implication is that your eyelids are the peel," Brandy told her. "So by peeling your eyes, you're opening them."

"Why not just say 'Keep your eyes open,' then? Makes a lot more sense than peeled."

"If old sayings made sense," Scott ventured, "they probably wouldn't be so memorable. 'A stitch in time saves nine'? It'd be just as easy to say something like, 'Hey, better fix that before it gets worse.' I mean, why nine? Because it sort of rhymes with time, only not really?"

"Yeah," Brandy put in. "Or 'One bad apple ruins the whole bunch.' Does it really? And if it does, how long do you have to leave it in there before they're all ruined? If you leave it long enough, is it really that apple ruining it, or just the fact that you've ignored your apples too long?"

"I thought it was 'One bad apple doesn't ruin the whole bunch,'" Rebecca said.

"Well, then," Brandy said, suitably chastened. "I guess that's different."

The road was hard to follow, and Scott let the conversation continue on without him while he gave all his focus to crawling forward, cutting through the drifted snow without losing the packed earth underneath. This direction led into a meadow scooped from the mountains as if with a shallow spoon. In spring it would probably be a riot of color as wildflower blooms filled its grassy expanse, but now it was just more white in a landscape of it. At the other side of the meadow, Scott could see where the roadway carved a notch through a stand of pines. The SUV growled as he pushed on and up, and a few minutes later they passed into the shade of the trees. There hadn't been much sun to begin with, and now that it was gone, a chill enveloped the vehicle. Scott shivered and cranked the heater up another notch.

He hoped his sudden chill was just from the temperature outside and not from anything else—not from any sense of foreboding that came from heading into the deep woods.

But he wouldn't have put money on it.

Somehow Christmas Day often seemed like the longest day of the year, although Kerry knew it wasn't. She supposed it must be the lack of pressing commitments. People didn't expect much of others on Christmas, most businesses were closed so there wasn't much reason to leave home, and relaxing was the order of the day.

In Season's New Hampshire refuge, the same rule applied. The witch had indicated that leaving would be almost impossible, so deep was the snow outside. After their morning talk, Kerry had taken a long bath, letting the hot water soak her completely. Then she had dressed, checked in on Season, and gone back to her room for a nap.

But sleep wasn't in the cards for her. She sprawled on the bed for a while, tossed and turned, tried to get comfy. But her mind was racing, everything Season had told her roiling around in it trying to find purchase. It seemed every time she believed she had a handle on how the world was really laid out, she discovered new information that completely redrew the map. *Christopher Columbus must have felt this way,* she thought. *Only sometimes I think I really am sailing right off the edge.*

When she needed grounding, needed to

reconnect to those things in her crazy life that seemed to truly make sense, she turned to Daniel Blessing. All she had left of him now were memories and his journals, so she took one of those heavy leather volumes from her duffel bag and slipped off the thong that held it closed. Turning a few pages, she found a passage she had never read.

> *The town wasn't much more than a flat spot where someone had scraped away the desert and built a couple of saloons, a church or three, a stable, a jail, and a random scattering of houses. I hadn't come for the scenery, however, or for the fine cuisine. I had come in search of a man named Stearns, who, I was told, had a score to settle with Season Howe, and maybe reason to know where she is. Seeing as I had a score or two of my own, I reckoned maybe we could be friends.*
>
> *When I rode in this afternoon, it was through brutal, punishing sun and heat. My horse was stumbling for the last half mile or so, even though I imagined he could smell the water waiting at the stable. I*

imagined that I could smell it too, and gave some thought to leaving the horse there if he fell and finishing the trip on foot.

Luckily, the horse held out. We covered that last stretch and made it to the relatively cool shade of the livery stable, where he dunked his muzzle into the trough and drank deep. It was all I could do not to join him, but I left him there and headed to the nearest saloon. A sign painted on the wall above the door said it was the Lucky Sack, but there wasn't much about it that looked lucky to me.

I had never let that stop me in the past, and wasn't about to now. I walked in out of the dusty late afternoon sunlight. A barkeep stood behind a plank balanced across two barrels, with a row of bottles and some glasses on a shelf behind him. Eight other men, mostly crowded around two tables but for a couple of lone drinkers, looked up when I entered. I suppose I must have looked like a threat—a stranger, rare in these parts to begin with, and one who carried a Colt strapped to his side. I almost never used the gun, of course. I had other, more effective weapons at my disposal. But I carried it to forestall any questions about why I wasn't armed, which had come up with depressing regularity until I'd bought this one.

I ordered a whiskey and a water from the barkeep, a portly fellow in a stained shirt and fraying suspenders holding up his britches. He put two glasses down in front of me without a smile. I did smile as I put my coins on his plank, overpaying by a wide margin.

"That's too much," he said.

"Not necessarily," I said. "You have rooms to let here?"

"Couple, upstairs. You might have to share."

"That's okay," I told him. I drank the water down, asked for another one. He brought it. This time he smiled a little, or at least his bushy mustache twitched.

"Anything else?" he asked.

Parched, I drained the second water. "Yeah," I said when I was done. "I'm looking for a man named Stearns. Know him?"

The barkeep blanched visibly. "Never heard of him."

"You always turn white when you hear a name for the first time?" I asked him.

"I didn't," he said. He turned away and started to wipe out glasses with a filthy rag.

"You did," I said. "And I hope you didn't dry these glasses with that thing."

"Look, mister, you don't like the way I do business, you can just move along."

"I got nothing against your business practices," I said, which wasn't entirely true. "I just don't like being lied to."

When he came back over to me his voice was low and the look on his face was surly. "I don't need the trouble, okay?" he said with a snarl. "Sayin' that name out loud around here is like askin' for a fight to start."

"One starts, I'll finish it," I said softly. "Just tell me where I can find this Stearns."

He looked around like he was afraid someone would jump him if he talked to me, and then he leaned closer, still wiping out a glass with that rag. "I couldn't tell you if I wanted to," he whispered. "People don't find Stearns. He finds them."

"What does that mean?" I asked.

"Either he lives somewhere around here or he doesn't."

"That's what you'd think," the barkeep said. "But it ain't always the truth."

I couldn't figure out what he was talking about, but I knew better than to push too hard. Surely few knew better than I that things weren't always what they seemed, and that sometimes asking questions only revealed answers that you didn't really want to know.

"So just by asking you about him, he'll come to me?"

"If he wants to," the barkeep answered. "He don't do things he don't want to do, way I hear it."

"A man of mystery."

"Don't laugh about him," the barkeep warned me. "Way I hear it, he don't like that."

"Well, give me a room then," I said. "I'll have some dinner and then see if old Mr. Stearns pays me a visit."

And I did just what I said I would. I wandered around the town, what there was of it, for a little while. Ate some *stringy steak and biscuits for dinner, and then went up to the room, which in fact I didn't have to share. And I waited. Eventually, I slept.*

I didn't even hear him come into the room, which is rare for me. I woke up when I heard the click of his revolver. When I opened my eyes he was pointing it at me.

"You must be Stearns."

"What makes you think so?"

"I was told if I looked for you, you'd find me."

He smiled. The room was dark but there was some moonlight leaking in through a window, and I could see that he was lean and rangy, with a droopy mustache and some gold in his teeth. His eyes were narrow and dark, and I had the feeling they didn't miss much. The pistol in his hand looked like it had seen plenty of use. There was no shake there, either, like there usually would have been when someone snuck into another man's room and pointed a gun at him. Mr. Stearns was just as calm as he could be.

"Why were you looking?" he asked.

"We have a mutual acquaintance," I said. I sat up a little in the bed now, my hands spread on the blanket in front of me so he could see I wasn't making a play for the Colt. "Name of Season Howe."

"Not sure I know that name," he said.

"No one around here seems to know anyone else," I said. "You don't have to worry that I'm a friend of hers or anything. I aim to kill her."

Stearns smiled at that, uncocked his gun, and slid it into his holster. "Well, why didn't you say so?" he asked. "What do you call yourself?"

I told him my name. He nodded slowly, as if he had to think on it for a while. "What's your gripe with Season Howe?" he asked after a bit.

"Let's just say she owes a price that's bigger than she can pay in this lifetime," I said. Not knowing Stearns, I didn't want to go into detail.

"That's true," he said. "You don't know the half of it."

"I know enough."

"Sounds like you've really got it in

for her," Stearns said. "I like the sound of that. And I can see you're a man who can handle her."

This man Stearns was full of surprises. "What makes you say that?"

"Well, being a witch and all, I mean. Same as her, that's all."

Which was what I thought he was getting at, but I didn't expect he'd come right out and say. He said it without hesitation, like he just knew it was true. So I didn't see any reason to deny it. I just sat there on that uncomfortable slab of a bed staring at him.

"You're wondering how I know," Stearns said. "Can't blame you." He moved closer to me, tilting his head up toward the ceiling. Beneath the edge of his whiskers I could clearly see the raw, choppy line where his throat had been cut. "I got a score to settle too, but I can't do it by myself," he said. To demonstrate further, he reached toward my bed, but his hand passed right through it with no resistance.

"I can see how that might be a problem for you," I admitted.

"Reckon you'll have to set things right for both of us," he said. "I can tell you where to find her—information is easy to come by on this side of the divide. She's in Durango. I don't know for how long, so I'd be on my way in the morning if I was you."

I was going to say something else, but didn't. Next thing I knew, I was waking up at first light. The whole thing might have been a dream—there's no sign that Stearns was ever here at all. So I'm putting this down just as it happened, in case I forget any of the details later.

After I get some breakfast in me, I'm lighting out for Durango. I have a feeling it wasn't a dream.

And I have a feeling that if I pass the town cemetery on the way out and look at the markers there, I'll see one with the name "Stearns" on it.

I remain, Daniel Blessing. Twentieth of July, 1871.

Kerry closed up the book and put it back in her bag. She knew there was a long tradition of ghost stories at Christmas—even the old chestnut "A Christmas Carol" was a ghost story, after all. This one she would once have read as a ghost story and felt a little shiver at, but knowing that Daniel had put it down—and that, at least when he wrote it, he believed every word he wrote—gave her a serious case of the creeps. Sure she had seen plenty of strange and spooky things over these past few months, but this little tale struck her as especially frightening.

Still, somehow she couldn't help feeling a little encouraged by what she had read too. There were times when she felt like she was the only person who was constantly surprised by others—like she just didn't have a handle on who people were and how they acted. She was glad to know that Daniel could be fooled too.

Maybe she hadn't been wrong to trust Mother Blessing. At least until she showed her true colors. Lacking evidence that someone presented themselves as something other than what they were, a person could go crazy not trusting anyone. *And where,* she wondered, *would that get you? That's probably why people become hermits—living in caves because they just don't know who they can believe and who they can't.*

Kerry preferred to trust first, and doubt, if there was a reason to, later. She had doubted Season—with perfectly good reason—but now that seemed to be turning around. Would it turn into trust? No telling yet. But that possibility was open now, where it wouldn't have been even a few days before.

She thought that, in some way, Daniel might approve.

14

Scott kept cranking the heat higher and higher, but the air outside grew colder as the afternoon dragged on. Brandy zipped up her coat and shoved her hands into her fleece gloves. But she didn't get really nervous until Scott said, "You know what would really stink? Running out of gas up here."

"Yeah, that would stink, all right," Rebecca agreed. "Does running your heat use extra gas?"

"I know running the air conditioning does," Scott said. "I guess heat probably does too."

"Turn it off, then, if you're getting low," Brandy urged.

"But we'll freeze," Scott protested.

"We'll freeze if we run out of gas," Brandy

countered. "Or have you seen a service station that I missed somewhere in the last hundred miles or so?"

"We haven't gone anywhere near that far," Scott said.

"I'm talking square miles."

"Okay," Scott said, beginning the complicated process of turning around on a narrow, snowbound road. "It's getting late anyway, and we don't want to be caught up here after dark."

"I sure don't," Rebecca said.

Brandy didn't answer. She was trying not to give Scott a hard time, but she felt like the day had been mostly wasted. They had cruised through the woods, up and down whatever little dirt roads they could find beneath the snow. But there was no rhyme or reason to it, no actual plan beyond just looking and keeping their fingers crossed. They hadn't seen any buildings or stray Jeeps, but New Hampshire was a big place, and not far from here was the Canadian border.

She had gone along with the day's agenda—or lack thereof—so she couldn't blame anyone but herself. Now it would be night soon, and their search would be ended until tomorrow. Who knew what could happen in that time?

Merry Christmas, Kerry, she thought bitterly. *Sorry we failed you.*

But tomorrow, she swore, would be different. Tomorrow they would use their heads, would approach the problem logically. "No more of this driving aimlessly," she said. "Soon as it's light, we've got to get smart about finding Kerry."

"You have any ideas, Brandy?" Scott asked. "Because you didn't when I was looking for some earlier."

"Maybe I do," Brandy replied. "I was thinking: If we were the police, we wouldn't look for a missing person by driving around the neighborhood, would we?"

"I guess not," Scott said.

"Of course not. We'd ask questions. We'd investigate. That's what we'll do tomorrow— we'll hit the little towns around here and see if anyone knows Season, or if anyone's seen her. If she's hiding out in this area, then she must buy food from someone. If she has a place to live, she must have bought or rented it from an agency or somebody like that. So we ask around."

"I like it, Brandy," Rebecca said. "It makes sense to me."

"Can I just remind you both that she's a witch?" Scott shot back. "We don't know if she needs a grocery store, or if she can just conjure up a meal from thin air."

"Well, she'd have to buy gas, then. Something. At least it's a chance," Brandy insisted. "It's better than trying to cover a million square miles of wilderness."

"Do you think we should call in the real authorities?" Rebecca suggested. "I mean, if Kerry's been kidnapped for real, maybe we should be getting the FBI or the National Guard or something after her."

Brandy snorted. "You want to try to explain Season to the New Hampshire state police? You're gutsier than me."

"Yeah, okay, maybe that wouldn't work," Rebecca admitted. "But it just seems like we need some, I don't know, reinforcements or something."

"Reinforcements would be great, but I wouldn't hold my breath," Scott said. "I think we're it."

"What about Mother Blessing?" Brandy asked. "Could we ask her for help somehow?"

"I don't think we'd want to do that," Rebecca cautioned. "It sounded like she and Kerry had kind of a falling out."

"But she still hates Season, right?" Brandy pressed. "We were talking about stupid old sayings earlier, and 'The enemy of my enemy is my friend' fits into that."

"You were wrong about the apple one," Scott reminded her. "What if you're wrong about this one too? What if it's something like, 'The friend of my enemy is my enemy'?"

Brandy shrugged. They were on their way back down the hill, coming out of the trees, but still a long way from civilization. The sun was a pale copper ball perched at the crest of the mountains. "Same idea," she said. "Mother Blessing and Season are enemies. Season has Kerry. Anyone who could help, I think we ought to consider."

"Yeah, but Beck and I have had more time than you have with Kerry recently," Scott argued. "She didn't give me the whole scoop—you know how she's been, always holding stuff back—but I got the same sense that Rebecca did. Kerry and Mother Blessing didn't part on the greatest terms."

"Whatever," Brandy said, throwing up her hands. Here she was intentionally trying not to ignite some kind of great debate, but she was in the middle of one anyway. All she wanted was to make sure Kerry was safe. Then she would make the argument that what they really needed was to leave Season alone, to stop this crazy hunt for her. Sure, there was a chance that Season was after them. They continued to get mixed up with her because they were worried about that possibility. But realistically, if they just went about their own business, ignored Season, wouldn't she do the same to them? They weren't really a threat—that had been proven time and again.

She didn't know how the others would feel about it. She wasn't even really sure if she cared any more. She missed Adam, she missed her family. It was Christmas! And instead of celebrating her favorite holiday of the year with loved ones, she was traipsing all over the White Mountains with her ex-boyfriend and someone she had known for one summer.

That was messed up.

"Okay," Scott said as he urged the SUV onto yet another ribbon of trail. "Tomorrow we do it your way, Brandy. We'll hit the towns, question the local yokels. Anybody have a picture of Kerry? It'd be easier if we had one of Season, but anything is better than nothing, right?"

"No picture here," Brandy said.

"I have one on my Web site," Rebecca offered.

"You have a Web site?"

"I've just been working on it the last couple of weeks," she said. "Kerry bought me a digital camera, and I've been putting up some pictures."

"That's just peachy," Brandy said. "So all we have to do is go into the grocery stores and gas stations and ask people to browse the net for a while."

"No, silly," Rebecca answered. "We just need to find a computer that we can print from. Maybe one of the hotels around has a business center, or there's an Internet café or something around."

"At the risk of starting another bizarre digression," Scott said, "we'll be going through a few towns on the way back to the condo. Everybody keep your eyes peeled."

Kerry and Season bundled up and went for a walk in the woods. The bitingly cold air smelled freshly scrubbed, the snow crunched loudly underfoot, and a few of the hardier birds whistled and fluttered from branch to branch overhead. The sun hung in the sky like a decoration, with no discernible purpose, since Kerry couldn't tell any difference in temperature between shade and bright sunlight.

"This is what winter should be like, to me," Season said. "I've spent plenty of them in warmer climes, but I can never get used to listening to Christmas music while the palm trees sway, or going out in January in shorts and sleeveless tops. It just seems wrong to me."

"I wouldn't mind the chance to find out," Kerry said. "I kind of liked the couple of weeks I spent in Santa Cruz. And Rebecca said it's relatively cool there because it's right on the water and everything—back down in San Diego, she said, it'd be a lot warmer."

"That's true. And down in Baja, or the Florida Keys, it's warmer still. But it's just not winter to me. I guess I'm old-fashioned or something. I think winter should be the time you put on a lot of clothes, drink hot chocolate or eggnog, and complain about the cold."

"And go sledding," Kerry added. "Sledding's good. I haven't done it since I was a kid, but . . ." She waved a hand toward a slope that faced them through the trees. "That'd be a great spot for it."

"You're right," Season agreed, a broad smile on her face. "Shall we?"

Kerry looked at her for a moment, confused. "But . . . with what sleds?"

"Kerry," Season said, shaking her head sadly. "Witches, remember?" She spoke one of the old words and gestured toward the slope. Kerry saw a faraway flash of light, and then two colorful objects appeared against the white snow.

"Sleds?"

"Flexible Flyers," Season confirmed.

"I am so there." Kerry broke into a run, and Season started in right behind her. When she was a kid, back in Cairo, there had been a street near her house that was steep and straight. On winter weekends the residents there closed the street off and ran hoses down it, icing it up, making a sled run out of it. There was always the unhelpful neighbor who left a car or truck parked at the curb, but most pulled into driveways or garages to clear the path. Someone would build a bonfire at the top of the hill at night, and the adults would gather around it for drinks and conversation while the kids sledded. Kerry had spent many happy winter hours streaking down that hill, and the few frightening moments, when her sled was caught on the ice and seemed determined to plow her into one of the parked cars or a fellow sledder, just made the whole experience that much more memorable.

A few minutes later Kerry huffed her way up to the top of the slope, leaving a trail of deep bootprints in her wake. The sled she found looked brand-new, but at the same time it looked like one that had hung high up in her parents' garage when she'd been little—supposedly it had been her dad's when he was a kid. It was made of blond wood slats with red metal rails, and it had the familiar arrow logo in the middle.

"This is great!" she shouted when Season caught up.

"Take her out for a spin," Season suggested.

Kerry hesitated for just a second, part of her still looking for the trap, the angle. She had been at war with Season. Could this be for real? But then she felt the combination of sun warm on her face and snow cold at her feet. That was real. The sled felt real, too. She grabbed its edges, ran a few steps, and then hurled herself on top of it as it rocketed down the slope. The sled gained speed as the hill grew steeper. Wind pummeled Kerry's face, snow flew as she sliced through it. A shriek behind her told her that Season was on her way down too.

At the bottom of the slope, she had to turn away from a couple of large rocks jutting up through the snow, and then from a creek that carved through the valley. She ended her ride in a spray of snow and a fit of laughter.

Season rolled her sled at the hill's end, and she came up laughing hysterically. "That was so fun!" she shouted. "This was such a good idea, Kerry!"

"I know!" Kerry called back. She was already using the attached length of rope to drag her sled back up the hill for another ride, her earlier moment of paranoia almost—but not completely—shoved away. Season caught up to her on the climb.

"I'm so glad you thought of this, Kerry. It's been a long time since I've done something just for fun."

"If I was a witch I'd do fun stuff all the time," Kerry replied.

Season grabbed her arm. "If?"

Kerry realized what she meant. She did not yet always think of herself as a witch, even though she'd been trained by Mother Blessing and could do things far beyond the abilities of most other people. To hear Season confirm her status somehow carried a lot of weight with her. "Yeah, okay," she said. "I guess I am a witch. But I've been kind of, you know, preoccupied." *With killing you,* she thought but didn't say. She was sure Season understood that anyway.

"Me too," Season said. "Having to be on edge all the time, literally for centuries . . . it interferes with my enjoyment of things."

Kerry nodded. "Even before—before I met Daniel and got all mixed up in this, I had kind of given up on fun," she admitted. "I was too busy taking care of Mom, and then going to school, working . . . I kind of let fun go by the wayside."

They had just reached the top of the slope. Season threw her sled down to the snow. "So let's go again!" she cried, pushing off and starting her trip.

Kerry spun and started hers as well, shooting down the hill behind Season.

Later they sat in Season's living room, nursing cups of hot chocolate. Kerry's cheeks were chapped, and they hurt from smiling so much and laughing so hard, but the fire and the warm beverage helped. They had sledded until the sun started to slide behind the hills, staining the snow as surely as if someone had spilled a bucket of red ink on it, and the air turned so cold that both were shivering almost uncontrollably. Kerry noticed near the end that her sled was literally breaking down—its hard edges softening, becoming less distinct, bits of it just disappearing from view. Season explained that most magically created items couldn't last very long—they were made by repurposing other materials, which needed to return to their original state before too long. Food was an exception to that rule; it was composed of tiny bits of organic material from so many different sources that they weren't missed.

At a quiet moment in the conversation, Season offered Kerry a gentle reminder. "You have five questions left. Do you still want to use them?"

Kerry had been turning things over in her mind, trying to narrow down what she wanted to ask about. But her major questions had already been answered, and the rest of it seemed small-time compared with the things she'd asked earlier.

"Okay," Kerry said after contemplating awhile. "We were talking about having fun earlier, and I know you have tended to hide out in resort-type areas. Daniel said it's because the population in those places changes a lot, swelling during their main seasons, so you can come and go without really being noticed. And I know you were in Las Vegas in the fall, because that's where Josh saw you. I also know you were in a casino on Samhain, which, I've got to tell you, really ticked off Mother Blessing. So what I want to know is, what is a witch doing in a casino on the holiest night of the year?"

Season considered her answer only briefly. "I'm not surprised that Mother Blessing was perturbed by that," she said. "She likes to make a big issue of being all traditional. When, of course, if she was truly that traditional she would never have done the things she did, back in Slocumb or since."

"Like what?" Kerry asked, before realizing what she was saying. *Another one down.*

"Witches aren't evil by nature," Season replied. She had changed into a soft cream-colored sweater and brown pants, but in honor of Christmas her socks were red and green striped. Once again she sat on a rug on the floor, leaning on the hearth, where her mug rested. "Or at least we're not supposed to be. Most of us are not, but there is a minority that are—that's why the natural slide toward entropy, or chaos, is so hard to resist. It was not traditional of her to allow the deaths of children that she could have prevented. It was not traditional of her to put me in the awful position of having to kill my own grandsons. But let me go out for an evening's entertainment, and she's offended?

"Samhain is, in fact, a holy night to most witches," Season went on. "And it's perfectly appropriate to celebrate it with ritual and solemn observance. But it's also fine to celebrate it with a party, or by having a good time in some other way. There is no single way that Samhain must be observed, regardless of what Mother Blessing might say. I paid attention to Samhain in my own way, and part of that was going to a casino—the closest thing there is to a truly holy place in money-worshipping Las Vegas—to enjoy myself. And was attacked by her simulacra. Surely she knew I was there because your friend called you."

Which means, Kerry extrapolated, *that I got Josh killed. If it hadn't been for me, Mother Blessing would never have known where to send the artificial men who killed him.* The realization hit her like a truck. *Good thing she doesn't know where Season is now, or I'd be in real trouble.*

"Can I—I mean, I'd like to save the rest of my questions for another time," Kerry said. Her sudden insight depressed her, and she felt very tired. "If that's okay. I think I'm ready to call it a night."

"If that's what you want, Kerry."

"Yeah, I think so. But thanks for a great Christmas, Season."

Season appeared to be unexpectedly touched by Kerry's sentiment. She swallowed, and her hand went to her chest. "Thank you," she said. "I hope I've cleared some things up for you."

"A lot," Kerry assured her. "Doesn't mean I don't still have a long way to go. But you've helped."

"Good night then, Kerry. I'll see you in the morning."

Kerry wished Season a good night, and then retired to her room.

Kerry Profitt's diary, December 25.

Well, that was certainly one of the strangest Christmases ever.

A fantastic one, for the most part. If you don't count the lack of a tree with presents underneath it. Which I kind of do, but I'm trying to look beyond that.

Anyway, there's more to life than presents and material things. Back when I was mall-happy I'd never have believed I would ever think that. And the truth is, even though I'm snowed into this cabin with no one around but Season, I still put on clean under-wear today, and socks, and did my makeup, and brushed my hair. Not that good grooming is neces-sarily the same as being materialistic, but I guess what I'm saying is that I'm not going all Flintstones or anything. More like Gilligan's Island, I guess, where the women had plenty of clothing and makeup even though they were only going on a three-hour tour.

And what would life be without old TV references to keep us sane? Thank the Goddess for TV Land, I say.

Well, enough of that. And enough digressing, keeping me from the main point of this little dia-tribe, which is . . .

. . . is . . .

First of all, I really can't remember the last time I just let loose and laughed like that. I guess some of those nights at home with the La Jolla gang, when Mace would start complaining about modern life and our strange back-east ways, and then Scott would go off on him—all in fun, of course, but fun with an edge to it.

So the walk in the snow, and the sledding, and the fact that we didn't have to drag our sleds home because they never really existed somehow . . . I don't quite get that, but at least no trees had to die for our enjoyment—that was all great.

So was the other part, in a different way. Just relaxing with Season, getting some questions answered. I am horrified—just wrenched apart—by the idea that I got Josh killed. I couldn't have known, of course. I trusted Daniel's mother. My mistake.

And now, it seems, I am starting to trust Season. Another mistake? I already know she's a murderer, so the answer should be a resounding "Duh!" But maybe it's my own naïveté. . . . I can't bring myself to doubt her when she speaks so frankly. She could be telling me one lie after another. Without evidence to the contrary, I just don't know. I'm reminded of those first days with Daniel, when I trusted him instinctively, or so I thought, but I found out later that, in fact, he had enchanted us.

We always say we are "enchanted" by people to whom we feel an instant, inexplicable attraction. Maybe we are, but that kind of enchantment is different from this kind—less manipulative, I guess. A matter of chemistry and pheromones and personal taste.

I don't know that Season has intentionally enchanted me. But I don't know that she hasn't.

Is trusting her some kind of betrayal of Daniel? Or of my vow to avenge his death? Should I go in there right now and just kill Season? I'm sure she trusts me enough now to let me get close. One of those carving knives, from the kitchen. It would be over in a second, except for cleaning up.

But would it be the right thing to do? Not just because she killed Daniel, but in the greater scheme. And listen to me (well, okay, read me), thinking about the greater scheme. Like my actions can affect the whole world.

Except, to hear her tell it, maybe they can. Which means I have to think before I act.

I hate that.

I also hate not knowing who to trust.

I guess I've got to stay on my guard. If I catch Season in a lie, or turn up something that proves she isn't telling the truth, then I call her on it. Or I make like a tree and "leaf." Except around here, most of the trees are pines and so the bad pun doesn't even work. Unless needles are leaves, in which case . . . oh, never mind.

It would be so much easier if . . . if it was easier. Same could be said for the rest of life, right? Think it ever is?

Me neither.

More later.

K.

15

Berlin had a copy shop with Internet connections, but it didn't open until ten, so they got a late start on their day. Rebecca brought up her Web site and saved the photo of Kerry—really of the two of them together, taken by Erin on one of the few occasions she had been around while Kerry had been visiting. Erin had a new boyfriend, and she'd been spending most of her time at his place, leaving Rebecca in the house alone. She had loved having Kerry visit, because she didn't like being home by herself—didn't like being anywhere by herself, she had realized. Being by herself just gave her too much time to think.

Once the photo was downloaded, it was an easy matter to crop herself out. She wanted the picture to show just Kerry, to keep any confusion to a minimum when they started spreading it around. It was a small file, fine for online viewing, but it printed blurry and grainy. Still, Kerry's pale skin, long dark hair, and huge green eyes were visible. They had been in Rebecca's kitchen, and there was a yellow wall behind Kerry that set her off nicely.

The first person they showed it to was named Frank, according to the tag on his shirt. He worked in the copy shop, and Rebecca slid it across the counter while Scott paid for the computer time. "Have you seen this girl?" she asked. "She might be with an older woman, a very pretty blonde."

Frank looked at the picture for a long time—maybe taking some time to admire as well as checking to see if he recognized her. "Nope," he said after a while. "Think I'd remember her."

"Okay, thanks," Brandy said, snatching the picture away.

They went outside onto Berlin's main drag—mostly brick buildings, very traditionally New England-styled. Here and there a cupola or clock tower broke the rooflines. Many businesses were closed, their storefronts boarded over or shuttered up. Signs for commercial real estate agencies hung on most of them, but they looked like they'd been there a long time. Rebecca remembered a mill they had seen on the river the day before—empty and abandoned, like a ghost town. For a minute she had thought it looked that way because of Christmas; no one would be working the mill on Christmas. But a closer look proved that to be false: The parking lots were blanketed in untouched snow, the buildings had broken-out windows and caved-in walls.

They tried a restaurant, a coffee shop, a drugstore, a gas station, but in each place they had the same response. No one remembered having seen Kerry or recognized the description of Season.

Finally, after searching for more than an hour, they reached the office of Bald Cap Realty and pushed through the heavy glass door. An old heater made the air smell stale. There were two people inside sitting at desks behind a long wooden counter. The woman looked up first— fiftyish, lean and bespectacled, with brown curls framing her pinched face. "Can I help you?" she asked, her tone suspicious. *No way do we look like we're shopping for a house,* Rebecca realized.

"We're wondering if you've seen someone," Brandy began.

Rebecca put the photo down on the
counter. "This person," she said. "Or another
one. They might be together."

Scott took over. "The other one is a pretty
blonde, older than the girl in the picture. Mid-
thirties, maybe. Striking blue eyes, the kind you
don't forget. They're not from around here, so
you'd have noticed their accents, maybe."

"That sounds familiar," the man said, rising
from his own desk. He was younger than the
woman, but not by much. Round and balding,
but with a gray beard hugging his chin. He
buttoned his red blazer as he approached the
counter, seemingly out of long habit. "An
attractive blonde, you say?"

"What is this about?" the suspicious
woman asked.

"We're afraid they might be in trouble,"
Brandy said, repeating the line they had agreed
on in case anyone asked. "We haven't heard
from them in several days, but we know they
had a place around here."

The man looked at Kerry's picture. "Haven't
seen her," he said.

"The older one was here first," Scott interjected. "This one just came a couple of days ago."

"You remember, Margaret," the man said. "Couple years ago, that property up by Mount Cabot?"

"Hush, Steven," the woman called Margaret said sharply. "Why don't you young people go to the police if you think there's something wrong?"

"We don't really know if it's as bad as all that, ma'am," Rebecca said. "We'd hate to get everybody stirred up if it turns out to be nothing."

"But if you know where on Mount Cabot," Brandy added, "we'd sure appreciate a tip."

"We have nothing more to tell you," Margaret said.

"Okay, then, thanks for all your help," Scott said sarcastically.

As they left the office, Rebecca tried to remember where Mount Cabot was on their map. It wasn't much to go on, but it was better than they'd had before.

"Are you crazy?" Margaret fumed after they had left. "Don't you remember what she said?"

"Not exactly," Steven admitted. "What was it?"

"She paid us both an extra ten percent if we'd promise to keep quiet about her buying that place."

Steven sighed. "That was two years ago," he said. "I'm sure she just meant for a while, not forever."

"It was three," Margaret said. "And she didn't put any time limitations on it. Maybe you don't take your commitments seriously, but I do."

"Look, I'm sorry, Margaret. I didn't think it was a big deal, and I forgot." Of course it *was* a big deal to Margaret—it was always a big deal when anyone let her down in any way, or revealed that they were merely human. Margaret liked to think of herself as godlike, while everyone around her failed in their attempts to achieve her exalted level. Steven thought it was probably difficult to go through life surrounded by abject failures and the willfully unkempt, but Margaret seemed to thrive on her demonstrated superiority over all beings.

"Well, I just think you would keep the desires of our customers in mind," Margaret huffed.

Before Steven could answer, the door opened again. *Probably those same kids coming back for something they forgot,* he figured. He hadn't expected much business the morning after Christmas. He was surprised they were willing to brave Margaret again, but if they were he had to give them credit.

But when he turned back toward the door, it wasn't the kids at all, or anyone else that he had ever seen. It was two men—*well, things that are like men, anyway,* he corrected. They were mostly brown, the brown of the mud by the banks of the Androscoggin River, and slick like that mud, but there were other components as well. He thought he recognized the spokes of a bicycle wheel, a crushed aluminum soft drink can, and a plastic bag from a supermarket mixed in with the river mud. They wore no clothing, just mud from head to foot.

Then he blinked, because he couldn't really be recognizing those things, that made no sense at all. It was just because the men were coming in from outside and the light was behind them, that was it. He was about to rub his eyes and say something when Margaret screamed.

"It's—it's all right, Margaret," Steven said. When he addressed the . . . the *things,* he tried to sound forceful, but his voice caught and it came out squeaky and uncertain. "Look here, what do you want?"

One of them came forward and leaned its fists down on the wooden counter. Steven was sure he could see mud squish out from between its fingers, but then suck back in somehow. He felt a chill that went to the core of his being.

The thing spoke then, and its voice was surprising. Not in its inhumanity, he expected that. But this was at once inhuman and yet feminine, in some way, like this creature was only a speaker box for a female talking through it remotely. "Season Howe," the strange voice said. "Where is she?"

"I don't—I don't know who you mean," Steven said. He knew full well, but how could these bizarre man-shaped concoctions know that?

"Season Howe," the thing said again.

Margaret had begun to sob as soon as her initial scream died, and she was still sobbing now, sitting in her desk chair with her face buried in her hands. Through the sobs, she said, "She's the one those kids were looking for, you fool. On Mount Cabot. Just tell them what they want to know, get them out of here."

The thing leaning on the counter, the mud-man, looked into Steven's eyes with an eye that was nothing more than a thumb-sized space in his crudely sculpted head. There seemed to be some kind of intelligence there just the same, Steven thought. He would go to his grave believing that the thing read him like a book. "I—I didn't recognize the name," he sputtered. "But she—she's right. Mount Cabot. That's where she is. Where her cabin is, anyway."

"Mount Cabot," it repeated, in that same semi-feminine voice.

"That's right," Steven said. He was terrified, afraid that he would lose control of himself at any moment, that these horrible creatures would drive him completely mad. He was a hair's breadth away from becoming a gibbering idiot, rolling into a ball and hiding in the footwell of his desk. "Mount Cabot. Now please, just go—"

Before he could finish the thought, the

thing came across the counter at him, moving fast and . . . and fluidly, not like a man but like a liquid, splashing itself at him. Margaret screamed again, and Steven saw that the other one was on her, arms swinging, fists pumping. Then Margaret was silent, and Steven felt a wet, slick hand contract on his own throat, felt muddy fingers clamp over his mouth and nose. He couldn't breathe, and when he tried he sucked mud in, inhaled it; it filled him up, and then it was over his eyes too, or the world had gone mercifully dark.

Six dead people. That was more than the town had seen in—well, ever, as far as Will Blossom knew.

Ordinarily there wasn't much a constable had to do to keep order in Berlin, New Hampshire. Not much crime. Most people didn't have much to steal, anyway, except the tourists and skiers who came during the season. They found themselves victimized from time to time, but Will didn't feel too bad about that. They left their car doors unlocked and their fancy stereos disappeared, that was too bad. He would rather it didn't happen, but the end result was that they usually bought new car stereos, sometimes before they even left town, and that was good for the local economy.

The town's only gang was a pack of punk kids who couldn't make the high school football team, smoked cigarettes, and pushed around smaller kids for their lunch money sometimes. At least that's what Chief Blossom liked to think. The truth, which he seldom allowed himself to contemplate, was that there were other things going on under the surface of the town that he didn't like or understand. Sometimes there were kids who wound up in the river, or on a hospital slab. Someone was responsible for that. He didn't know if it was a gang or simply random circumstance. But as long as it didn't affect most of the townspeople, he didn't push too hard on it.

He was understaffed, of course. Every law enforcement agency was these days. And there had been a little more crime since the last big mill on the river had closed. Someone stealing a few cans of food, a loaf of bread, those things he could overlook. Life was hard all around, and he didn't leave himself out of that equation. The less he had to do to claim his bimonthly paycheck, the better he liked it.

So this morning he was a very unhappy man. The phone in his office was ringing off the hook, and every time it did it brought more bad news. He had already been out of the office more than he'd been in it today. Carla, his dispatcher, had a stack of pink message slips in her hand when he came in this time, and she shoved them into Will's fist.

"More calls," she said. "I'd have called you on your wireless but I knew you were just about here. You're going out again, though."

He had been dreaming about the chocolate bar in his desk drawer and a Coke to wash it down with. "I don't want to go out," he protested, knowing it was pointless. This was going to be one of those days that didn't let up, and then it would lead into a week or more of the same—funerals and distraught family members and demands for answers. He would find those answers, one way or another.

"You got a big staff of investigators going to do it for you?"

"I'm going out again," he relented. "Where am I going?"

"Depends," Carla said. "You want to work

them in order of when they called in? Or maybe alphabetically?"

"In order," Will said.

"Then you're going to the Tas–T–Scoop, Virgil's Café, Notions 'n' Things, and Bald Cap Realty."

"I know that's the name of the mountain," Will said. "But doesn't it sound like something an actor would wear if he needed to be bald?"

"You're wasting time, Will."

"I'm delaying the inevitable, Carla," he protested. "That's different."

"In what way?"

He couldn't think of any. "Okay, maybe not. Anyone else needs me, call me."

He left the office to go back into his town. The town he was supposed to keep safe, and in which half a dozen people had already died today. Maybe starting last night, he amended, since he didn't know precisely what time the murders had started to occur.

The scary thing was, nobody had put it all together yet. Some people knew a victim or two, but no one outside of his department knew how many there were. When they did, it would be trouble. Panic. He didn't want that.

He just wasn't sure how to avoid it.

He drove down to the Tas-T-Scoop. Kitty Russell was there in her colorful uniform, with the little striped cap and everything. But her eyes were red and her nose was running, and she was shaking like a leaf in a nor'easter. Will got out of his car and walked over to where she sat on a bench in the dining area, pointedly not looking toward the counter.

"What's wrong, Kitty?" he asked, afraid he already knew the answer. "What happened?"

She tried to point to the Formica counter, but her muscles failed her and her arm fell limply to her side. "It's—it's Mr. Penrose," she said through her tears. "He—he—he's back there."

Will massaged her back for a moment. "I'll just take a look, Kitty. You stay right here. Everything's going to be okay. You're safe, I promise you that. Okay?"

"O—okay . . ." she said, without apparent conviction.

He left her and let himself through the opening into the kitchen area of the ice-cream parlor. *Who'd buy ice cream on a day like today anyway?* he wondered. *Penrose should have just stayed home, and let Kitty stay home too. They'd both have been better off.*

On the floor behind the counter he saw just what he expected to see—what he'd seen at every other stop this morning. Same as Hoot Buffington, and Sandra Cliff, and Nat Landers. Penrose was dead. His clothes were foul, muddy, and they stank like the Androscoggin on a hot day. Mud caked his chin and neck, dribbled from his slack mouth. His eyes were open.

He looked terrified, even in death.

Will Blossom shuddered. He was a little terrified himself.

16

Writing about TV shows in her journal the night before had made Kerry realize how much she missed television. That, and the fact that TV had been part of her family's Christmas tradition: Charlie Brown, the Grinch, Rudolph, *Miracle on 34th Street* and *Holiday Inn* and *A Christmas Story*. It had been just ages since she had sat down and watched TV. A couple of days at the hotel in Portsmouth, and not for months before that. Maybe she'd been too busy living her life to simply observe, but on some level she felt removed from the rest of the country because they had gone on watching while she had been doing other things. TV might be over-rated, but it helped define America in a very real way, and she missed that attachment to her fellow citizens.

Besides, being stuck up on this mountain with Season was starting to wear on her. She liked the sledding and the fireplace and the conversation, but she craved communication, connection. She wondered if there was some sort of plan. When would the roads open—or had they already? When would they come down from the mountain? And, maybe most important, how did her new perception of Season fit into her life? What came next?

In the morning, while Season slept in, Kerry tugged on sweats, tied her hair back, and scouted around the cabin. No telephone—and her own cell, she had determined long ago, had no signal up here—no radio, no TV. Even Mother Blessing had owned a TV.

But, Kerry remembered, *witch.*

She racked her brain for a long while, but couldn't come up with a spell that would make a TV appear where there was none.

While she dwelled on it, sitting on the living room couch with her ankles crossed, knees up, hands resting on knees and chin on hands, Season came in.

"Good morning, Kerry," she said. She looked warm and comfy in a man's loose-fitting corduroy shirt and soft, flared gray pants.

"Do you have a TV? Wait—does that count—no, strike that. I'm hoping that doesn't count as one of my remaining questions. I'm still not sure how these stupid rules are supposed to work."

"Rules can be stupid," Season agreed. "But often you'll find that the stupidest ones aren't so bad once you realize why they're there."

"That doesn't answer my . . . my not a question."

"I won't count it, okay? And the other answer is no, no TV. But if you'd like to watch some today, you can."

"I was just feeling a little, you know, cut off from the world. This hermit deal isn't so much me, I guess. I'd kind of like to talk to my friends, too."

"I think we can arrange both," Season said. "Let's have some breakfast first, and then we'll get on that." She went into the kitchen and Kerry got off the couch to follow her. She had come to like watching Season cook, although not as much as she liked the eating part.

Season cracked a few brown eggs into a bowl. "I think an omelet would be good today.

Sound all right to you? Maybe with biscuits and some fresh fruit."

"Sounds yummy," Kerry said. "Why—and I guess this one can count—why do witches like to cook so much? Mother Blessing did too, and even Daniel was a good cook. I mean, you could just kind of *poof!* and there's an entire meal, right?"

"I could, yes," Season agreed. "I think part of it may be that we enjoy the process, though. Most witches I've met are good cooks. It's not unlike witchcraft, when you get down to it. We take natural ingredients, combine them in a specified manner, and the end result is something that isn't what it was, something that's new and different and functional. A lot of spells work the same way."

"That makes sense, I guess."

Season's hands flew with practiced assuredness. Kerry was a pretty fair cook herself—she had taken over the culinary duties at home once her mom got too sick—but her repertoire was basic. Breakfast was far more likely to be cereal and toast than Belgian waffles, sausages, and strawberries cut into the shape of roses. Anyway, there were lots of choices of breakfast cereal. She hadn't counted them all, of course, but in her local supermarket if you stood at one end of the cereal aisle you could almost see the curvature of the Earth in the shelves. She figured you could easily eat cereal every day for the rest of your life, a different box at a time, and never have to repeat yourself because they'd just keep coming up with new ones. Soon the cabin was filled with wonderful aromas that pushed any thoughts of such basic foods from her head.

"So . . . what comes next?" Kerry asked as they ate Season's delicious food. She felt awkward about it, but knew the subject had to be broached sometime. "I mean . . . you know. With . . . all this? I guess I don't want to kill you as much as I used to."

"Well, that's a relief," Season said with a warm smile. "I don't want to kill you either. I really am not a killer by nature."

"I think I've figured that out," Kerry admitted. "It was hard, though. Took me a long time to accept."

"Understandable. You've been through a lot, and you've seen a lot of awful things. And we've been on the opposite sides of most of it.

I guess the only way to answer your question is to ask you one. What do you want? There's probably no reason you have to stay involved in any of this. You can go back to school, go on with your own life, and leave our little intrigues behind. At least that's what I'd do if it was my choice."

Kerry dwelled on that for a moment. Back to Northwestern? Back to live with Aunt Betty and Uncle Marsh? Neither of those choices had very much appeal. She was eighteen—not a little girl, barely an adult by society's standards—but without the hunt for Season, without Daniel, she was completely adrift.

"I've been thinking about it a lot," she said. "But I haven't come to any firm decisions. Part of me would like to keep studying witchcraft, I think. That's the only thing that has really interested me lately."

Season looked a little surprised by Kerry's comment. "I would think you'd want to leave it as far behind you as possible, as fast as you could. I don't want you to jump into anything without giving it a lot of thought. It's not so easy to do, and there are a lot of sacrifices that have to be made, especially if you're not born into the community."

"I get what you're saying," Kerry said. "But I don't know. It seems like something I'm good at. Maybe I could make some kind of contribution."

"You probably could," Season agreed. "More omelet?"

After Kerry had done the dishes, she came into the living room to see Season looking at a TV set that stood on the hearth. It wasn't plugged into anything, Kerry noted, but there was a picture on its screen just the same.

"Cable or satellite?" she joked.

"Astral plane," Season answered with a grin. "Much clearer reception."

She held a remote control that looked perfectly authentic to Kerry. Pointing it at the TV, she started clicking through the channels. "Anything in particular you want to watch?"

"I've been so out of touch I don't even know what's on any more," Kerry moaned. "And a million new CDs are probably out, by a thousand new bands I've never even heard of. And movies? Is Josh Hartnett even a star anymore?"

Before Season could answer, something on

the TV screen caught her eye. ". . . gruesome murders in Berlin this morning have authorities baffled. The early morning killing spree has left seven dead. Berlin police chief William Blossom has asked all residents to stay inside with their doors locked as much as possible, until more is known about who has committed these savage crimes . . ."

"Look," Season said in a hushed voice. The screen showed a reporter standing outside a café in what must have been Berlin. There were muddy handprints on the doorjamb behind him, and more tracks of mud on the ground. Season pushed a button on the remote and the screen froze, as if they were watching a DVD or TiVo, and not a broadcast with the word "Live" in the corner. She pushed another button—*That's some remote,* Kerry couldn't help thinking—and the picture zoomed in on the muddy footprints.

Mixed in with the mud, Kerry could see cigarette butts, stray leaves, bits of paper, and other detritus. "Is that—?" she began.

"Simulacra," Season said anxiously.

"But they're—they're killing people! Why would they do that?"

Season's voice was solemn, her brow

furrowed with concern. "That's what they're best at." She eyed Kerry for a moment, then shook her head. "Sorry," she added. "That was flip. This is serious, and you deserve a real answer. Here's what I think: Mother Blessing is using them to look for me. She has tracked me to this area somehow. Instead of coming herself, she's sent the simulacra to find me. But she doesn't want anyone who sees them to be able to tell anyone else about them."

"Usually when she's with one," Kerry remembered, "she uses a glamour to make sure no one really sees them."

"That's right," Season agreed. "From this distance, though, it would be all she could do to keep them animated. So she would command them to kill any witnesses after they got whatever information they could."

Kerry shuddered. Sometimes she forgot just how brutal Mother Blessing could be. "Can we stop them?"

"We have to try," Season said. "But we have to get down there, fast."

Scott, Rebecca, and Brandy had just reached the RAV4, parked at a curb a few blocks from the real estate office, when they saw the police car race down the street past them, siren blaring, roof lights flashing. Scott realized that they'd been hearing sirens around town for the last twenty or thirty minutes, but they had been so busy trying to track down any information about Season that they had barely paid any attention.

"I wonder what's going on," he said. He wasn't curious enough to want to backtrack and find out—he was more concerned with getting on to Mount Cabot and finding Kerry. So much time had gone by since she had disappeared; he had a horrible feeling, sitting in his gut like a lead weight, that they would be too late to help her. It had taken only seconds for Season to kill Daniel, and Daniel had been a much more formidable opponent than Kerry would be. The only saving grace was that Season had taken Kerry away, instead of just finishing her off on the spot—to Scott, that suggested that the witch had some use for Kerry. If so, Kerry might still be alive.

But every minute might count.

"Looks serious," Rebecca added. She nodded toward a nearby intersection, which an ambulance screamed through at top speed.

"None of our business," Scott said. He fished his keys from his pocket to open the SUV. But before he reached the door, a dark shape separated from the nearby building and lumbered toward them. It took Scott a moment to realize that the figure was dark not because of shadows—as soon as it peeled away from the building's face, it moved into bright sunlight—but because it was, top to bottom, rich brown mud, not flesh or clothes.

"Umm . . . Scott . . . ?" Rebecca's voice quavered with fear, and he knew she had seen it too. His own voice seemed to fail him, as if it were out of his reach somehow.

But Brandy stepped up, the only indication of her own emotions a barely noticeable shaking of her legs, like her knees wouldn't quite lock under her. "It must be a . . . what do you call them? Simulacra? One of Daniel's mother's . . . things."

The man-shaped creature continued toward them with its odd gait, and Scott found his voice. "What do you want?" he asked. The thing's arms were at its sides, and there was nothing sinister or threatening in its demeanor. But when it stopped a few feet from them, its head cocked as if listening for something, it didn't speak, didn't answer in any way. "Tell us what you want," Scott insisted.

Finally, the simulacrum uttered one word, in a raspy, high-pitched voice that didn't seem to match up with its large, bulky body. "Season."

The three of them stood in place, stunned by the being's statement. Scott realized they shouldn't be—Brandy was almost certainly right, this thing was a simulacrum, and they were Mother Blessing's creations. It was only natural that the creature would be looking for Season.

"Mother Blessing must have . . . I don't know, tapped our phones or something," he speculated. "Or she's keeping tabs on us somehow, anyway. So when we found out where Season is, she sent her simulacrum. I don't think he wants to hurt us, or he already would have."

"Are you—do you want to go with us? To find Season?" Brandy asked the thing.

"But remember," Rebecca put in, "Kerry said Mother Blessing was kind of crazy or something when she left. I'm not sure she's actually on Kerry's side."

"She's against Season," Scott reminded them. "That means she's okay with me right now. If we find them—when we find them—we're going to need whatever help we can get to fight Season."

"Season," the simulacrum repeated in the same strange voice.

"How did you find us?" Brandy asked.

"Season."

"Kind of a one-track mind."

"If Mother Blessing can 'see' through its eyes, then she might have recognized us," Rebecca guessed. "She probably knows what we look like."

"We're going to find Season," Scott told the creature. "Do you want to go with us?"

The simulacrum shambled toward the SUV, which Scott took as an affirmative. "I guess we have company."

"It—he can ride in back with me," Rebecca offered. Turning to it, she added, "You don't mind if I open the window a little, do you?"

Scott understood—the closer it came, the more odiferous he realized it was, with a smell like rancid fish. He wondered if he'd ever be able to clean his vehicle sufficiently after this. It left mud tracks on the ground with every step, and he was afraid that after sitting on his back seat for the hour or so it would take to get up to Mount Cabot and find Season there would be a permanent stain.

But cars were replaceable. Kerry wasn't. They all piled in, the simulacrum scrunching itself in next to Rebecca. As soon as it was seated its head drooped to its chest, as if it had gone to sleep. *That's fine,* Scott thought as he started the vehicle and pulled away from the curb. *It won't be needed again until we find Season. And then we're going to want it to have all the strength it can manage.*

As they drove out of town, more sirens split the morning air.

17

Season's Jeep roared easily through the half-melted snow of Christmas Eve's storm. Season had warned Kerry that if the simulacra were so close they might not be able to return to the cabin, so they had taken a few minutes to pack up necessary belongings and thrown their bags into the back of the vehicle.

"How do you think she could she have found us?" Kerry asked as they bounced down the snow-packed road away from the cabin.

"I don't know," Season said. Her knuckles were white on the steering wheel. "You didn't tell those friends of yours where we've been, did you?"

"I hate to shatter any illusions," Kerry replied, "but I don't even know where we've been. With the snow and everything, I was lost as soon as you left I-93. Anyway, at the cabin my phone didn't have any signal, so I couldn't have told them even if I wanted to."

"Well, somehow she figured it out," Season stated.

The "she," Kerry knew, was Mother Blessing. And Season was right; she might well have been looking for either of them, or both. The news report on the TV had been brief, but terrifying—if Mother Blessing was willing to let her simulacra kill half a dozen innocent people in one morning, she had stepped things up considerably. Maybe she knew that Season and Kerry were together, and she believed they might be forming an alliance. That would be something, Kerry was sure, that Mother Blessing would go to almost any lengths to stop.

And it intensified her sense that teaming up with Season was the right thing to do— that Mother Blessing, not Season, was the real enemy. The long struggle between them had taken too many lives, but it was Mother Blessing who pressed the issue, who wouldn't let up. Season's responses, Kerry had come to accept, had been mostly defensive. Running and hiding weren't the actions of an aggressor.

Season would be aggressive now, Kerry was sure. The set of her jaw, the determined way she muscled the Jeep around turns and over the unpaved road—everything Kerry saw pointed to a Season who was outraged and ready for anything. Finally, their wheels hit pavement, and Season stomped on the gas, hurtling the Jeep toward Berlin and the ultimate confrontation.

The beast in the back seat made Brandy nervous, but she knew that it would be an important ally in the confrontation to come. She, Scott, and Rebecca had no magic, no special powers. They could find Season and Kerry, and then . . . they could yell and scream at the witch, maybe throw rocks at her. That was about the extent of their ability to cause her harm.

With the simulacrum in tow, maybe they could succeed in freeing Kerry from Season's grasp. She knew Season had beat simulacra before, but at least it was *something. Which,* she reasoned, *is better than nothing.*

Scott raced toward Mount Cabot with a seriousness of expression that Brandy at once admired and despised. Clearly the danger to

Kerry was foremost in his mind, and it may not even have occurred to him that by trying to rescue her, all he was doing was putting the rest of them into equal jeopardy. She hadn't tried to dissuade him—besides understanding that the effort would have been pointless, she wanted to force a showdown too. She hated the idea that Season was taking them one by one, like a fox picking off sheep who wandered too far from the flock. They needed to present a united front, to let Season know once and for all that she had to face them together or leave them alone.

Stinky mud-man would help make their case. They didn't have much power, but they had powerful friends. Maybe that would be enough.

As they sped up the road, she noticed a vehicle coming toward them. Scott spotted it too, and, glancing at him, Brandy saw his eyes widen in surprise. "It's the Jeep!" he said, almost breathless.

"Season's Jeep?" Rebecca asked from the back.

"Looks like it," Scott said.

Brandy narrowed her eyes, trying to sharpen

her focus. There were at least two people in the oncoming Jeep, but that was all she could make out at this distance. Scott didn't wait for confirmation. He pulled the RAV4 over to the side of the road, off the pavement, and jumped out. Standing at the edge of the roadway, he flapped his arms like a crazed penguin trying to fly.

Twenty yards away, the Jeep pulled over. Its doors opened and Season and Kerry got out.

Kerry didn't look like a prisoner.

The two women started toward them. Kerry, Brandy saw, had a wide smile on her face. *She's all right, then,* Brandy thought happily. She realized how tense she'd been only when her tension started to dissipate at the sight.

But a dozen yards away, Season put a hand against Kerry's chest, holding her back, and pointed toward them. Both women's faces changed, expressions of joy becoming looks of concern. They stopped their advance and took what could only be defensive positions.

"Scott . . ." Brandy warned. He had already started toward them, but he read the body language and halted in his tracks.

"What—," he started to say, but he let the rest of it die in his throat.

Season's posture—and Kerry's—were unmistakable. They were ready for war.

The sight of Scott's RAV4 pulling off the road had made Kerry's heart leap. "There they are!" she shouted gleefully. "We have to stop!"

"Okay," Season said. "For a minute. Just long enough to bring them up to speed. Then we have to get into Berlin to find those simulacra before they hurt anyone else."

"Deal," Kerry agreed. Season halted the Jeep and they both tumbled out, heading down the slope toward Scott, Brandy, and Rebecca. *They all came,* Kerry thought, her heart swelling. *Those guys are the best.*

Then Season's hand was on her, and they both came to a dead stop. "Look," Season cautioned. "Simulacra."

At first glance, Kerry saw only one, unfolding itself from the back seat of Scott's ride. But it was alone only for a moment. As Kerry watched, more shaped themselves from the packed snow and dirt beside the road, from pine needles and stray leaves, from litter and the tread of a shredded tire and a hubcap someone had lost. They formed from the ground up, a head first, then, as more matter clung together, growing taller and broader until they each stood on two strong legs. There were two, then four, then ten, and finally an even dozen, standing around Kerry's friends.

No, she corrected herself, *standing* with *my friends. Allied with them.*

"They—," she began.

Season confirmed her unfinished statement. "They're with Mother Blessing now."

"But—they can't be."

"No one else uses simulacra like she does."

"But someone could," Kerry suggested.

"Could, maybe. They don't. That's just the way it is."

"That doesn't mean—"

"Kerry, we don't have time to argue. They are there with the simulacra. One came in their car. Don't deny what's right in front of you."

Kerry felt her voice catch in her throat. "What—what are we going to do?"

"We're going to fight," Season answered. Kerry recognized that she had already taken a defensive posture, ready for the simulacra to attack. "The only alternative is to die, and I'm not keen on that one."

"Don't hurt my friends," Kerry pleaded. "We have to talk to them, make them explain what's going on."

"I'll try," Season agreed. But then she didn't speak anymore, because the army of snowmen rushed toward them, a massive wave of human-shaped debris.

Season spoke a few words of the old tongue, and a sudden, violet glow formed around her hands, which crackled with power. Kerry caught on and echoed her. She felt the energy tingle as her own hands sparked and the glow surrounded them also. A scent like fresh watermelon in the summer filled the air. Neither witch waited for the simulacra to get any closer, but both blasted at them—Season first, Kerry close behind—with energy pulses that radiated from splayed fingers. Where the pulses hit, simulacra burst apart, snow and earth and other ingredients flying apart, returning to their pre-enchanted states.

But they moved fast, and before Kerry and Season could dispatch all of them, Kerry felt a hard-packed fist slam into her ribs. The simu-lacrum had charged in so quickly she hadn't even seen it come, focused as she was on a more distant target. She doubled over and it swung again, its heavy hand smashing into her face and driving her down into the snow. She tried to blast it but the distraction had dissipated her energy field. She started to say the old words again. The thing gave her no opportunity, though—it came at her again, this time kicking at her. She dodged the foot, barely, and tried to grab its leg, hoping to pull it off balance. It was too fast, and she too weak from the brutal beat-ing. She missed. It launched another kick that looked like it would take her head off.

Then the simulacrum blew apart, and Kerry, shielding her face from the sudden shower of snow and dirt, saw Season toss her a smile. "You owe me one!" Season shouted. "Now get back into the game!"

Season was surrounded by them, Kerry realized. The dozen that had initially formed had been joined by many more, a virtual army of the pseudo-men. Even Season was in danger of being overrun by them, and yet she had taken the time to save Kerry from one.

Kerry forced herself back to her feet, wincing at the pain in her ribs, the throbbing of her face. The determination that had earned her the nickname Bulldog filled her with a sense of purpose. "*Malificant!*" she shouted to the skies, raising her arms as if to grab a cloud. "*Konatifat benilias!*"

This time the glow wasn't confined to her hands, and the electrical sensation rippled through her whole body. Kerry had made herself a living weapon. She didn't hesitate, but unleashed her power on the simulacra, throwing off blast after blast. Each one found its target, blowing another simulacrum back to its component materials. She began with the ones closing in on her, and then turned to the ones surrounding Season. As she destroyed one after another, she felt herself reveling in the power she wielded, taking a kind of joy from the destruction of her unliving enemies.

When it was over, when no more simulacra rose from the ground, she felt almost let down. She relaxed, shook herself, let the power slip back into the universe from which she had called it, and saw Season doing the same. They went to one another and shared a quick embrace, and Season's whispered "You were great" brought Kerry a swell of pride she hadn't felt in a long time.

Then Kerry turned toward her friends, toward Scott, Brandy, and Rebecca, who still stood beside Scott's SUV.

She expected to see happiness written on those familiar faces, pleasure that their foes had been defeated, that she and Season had prevailed. The happiness of a reunion with old comrades. She hadn't seen any of them since she had sent Scott away, and she had known she was hurting him terribly when she did. She wanted to hug him, to let him know she hadn't meant any of it, was only concerned for his safety. She wanted to hug all of them, to enjoy the reunion, to get past the adrenaline rush of the battle in the company of friends.

That was what she expected.

What she saw instead was absolute terror. Rebecca shrank visibly under her gaze, crossing her arms over her chest and taking a step toward the vehicle. Brandy and Scott stood their ground. None of them spoke, but their faces said it all.

They were afraid of Kerry. After all they

had been through, all she had done for them
. . . now she horrified them. They had seen her
power—and her capacity for violence—and
instead of being impressed, or pleased, or
heartened, all it had done was scare them.

She had been one of them. Now she was
something else. Something . . . other.

Kerry had become a witch, and her friends
were frightened of witches. Who could blame
them, really, considering what they had seen,
what they knew?

But reasoning through it, understanding
their reactions, didn't make any of it any easier
to take.

Kerry thought that her wounded heart,
which had so recently begun to heal, would
finally break.

End of Book Three

JEFF MARIOTTE is the author of more than fifteen previous novels, including several set in the universes of *Buffy the Vampire Slayer, Angel, Charmed,* and *Star Trek*; the original horror novel *The Slab*; and more comic books than he has time to count—some of which have been nominated for Stoker and International Horror Guild Awards. With his wife Maryelizabeth Hart and partner Terry Gilman, he co-owns Mysterious Galaxy, a bookstore specializing in science fiction, fantasy, mystery, and horror.

He lives with his family and pets in Douglas, Arizona, in a home filled with books, music, toys, and other examples of American pop culture. More information than you would ever want to know about him can be found at www.jeffmariotte.com.

UGLIES
SCOTT WESTERFELD

Everybody gets to be supermodel gorgeous. What could be wrong with that?

In this futuristic world, all children are born "uglies," or freaks. But on their sixteenth birthdays they are given extreme makeovers and turned "pretty." Then their whole lives change. . . .

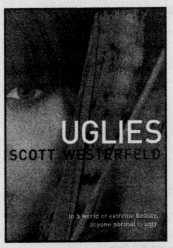

And coming soon: *Pretties*

PUBLISHED BY SIMON PULSE

the nine lives of chloe king

by **CELIA THOMSON**

**1 hero.
9 lives.
8 left.**

It happened fast. Just a moment earlier, Chloe had been sitting with Amy and Paul on the observation deck atop Coit Tower in San Francisco. *What would happen if I dropped a penny from up here?* she wondered. She climbed up on the railing and dug into her jeans pocket, hunting for spare change.

That was when she fell.

As Chloe tumbled through the fog, all she could think was, *My mother will be so upset when she finds out I skipped school. . . . Maybe all that stuff about your life flashing before your eyes is just bull.*

Or maybe Chloe already knew, down in the unconscious depths of her mind, that she still had eight lives to go.

Don't miss this hot new series from Simon Pulse:

The Fallen

The Stolen

The Chosen

Published by Simon & Schuster